The C

The glove was horribly real. You .... that cold, gripping hand. She knew now that something had reached out for her. Something had crossed over the boundary between worlds. Past and present, living and dead.

Sam is determined to prove that she can look after herself. After years of serious illness she has found herself a flat in Brighton, near the sea, and soon she will start looking for a job. Nothing is going to spoil things for her now.

But then frightening things start happening in her flat. One of the rooms seems to be possessed by the spirit of a long-dead girl and Sam hears her desperate crying in the night. Why has she come to haunt Sam? What terrible tragedy happened in the past to make her spirit so unhappy? Sam has to find the answers before it is too late, before her life, too, is ruined by what happened in that room all those years ago.

HAZEL RILEY was born in Gateshead and discovered a passion for reading as a child. That's when she decided she was going to be a writer. She studied English Literature at York University, becoming a Trotskyist, a radical feminist, and a Buddhist in rapid succession. After university she moved to London where she did a variety of jobs. She now lives in London with her dog and divides her time between teaching adult literacy and writing for teenagers. *The Crying* is her second novel for Oxford University Press.

The Crying

Other books by Hazel Riley

Thanis

The Crying

Hazel Riley

OXFORD
UNIVERSITY PRESS

OXFORD

UNIVERSITY PRESS

Great Clarendon Street, Oxford OX2 6DP

Oxford University Press is a department of the University of Oxford.
It furthers the University's objective of excellence in research, scholarship,
and education by publishing worldwide in

Oxford New York
Auckland Bangkok Buenos Aires
Cape Town Chennai Dar es Salaam Delhi Hong Kong Istanbul
Karachi Kolkata Kuala Lumpur Madrid Melbourne Mexico City Mumbai
Nairobi São Paulo Shanghai Singapore Taipei Tokyo Toronto

With an associated company in Berlin

Oxford is a registered trade mark of Oxford University Press
in the UK and in certain other countries

Lines from 'Rhapsody on a Windy Night' by T. S. Eliot from
Collected Poems 1909–1962, reprinted by permission of the publishers,
Faber & Faber Ltd.

The moral rights of the author have been asserted

Database right Oxford University Press (maker)

First published 2002

British Library Cataloguing in Publication Data available

ISBN 0 19 271915 7

1 3 5 7 9 10 8 6 4 2

Typeset by AFS Image Setters Ltd, Glasgow

Printed and bound in Great Britain
by Biddles Ltd, www.biddles.co.uk

For Connie

'And through the spaces of the dark
Midnight shakes the memory . . . '

from 'Rhapsody on a Windy Night' by T. S. Eliot

1

Sam heaved her suitcase halfway up the final flight of stairs. She was determined to do it on her own, not that there was anyone to help her anyway. Her heart was pounding with the effort and her muscles ached, but she didn't care. Pausing to catch her breath, she put her hand into her pocket and touched the big, old-fashioned key. The key to her new flat and to her new life. She could barely believe her luck at finding this place so cheaply. Big, sunny living room, two bedrooms, kitchen, and bathroom all to herself. It was a dream come true.

She bent down and picked the suitcase up again. She didn't look up until she'd reached the small landing at the top of the house. The key was already in her palm, but she didn't need it. The door was slightly ajar. She pushed it open uncertainly and called out, 'Hello, is anyone there?' Her voice echoed through the empty rooms then faded away. Only silence. 'Hello,' louder this time. Still nothing, but Sam had to fight off a strange feeling that she wasn't alone.

She closed the door softly, as if she were the intruder. Leaving her suitcase and shoes in the small cloakroom by the door she went into the living room and looked around. It was so sparsely furnished there was nowhere to hide. She stood and listened, but there was only the sound of her own breathing, slowly getting back to normal as she began to relax.

The living room opened into a corridor that stretched the length of the house and led to the kitchen and bedrooms. It seemed darker and more gloomy than she'd remembered. There were no windows, only a row of closed doors, but the air felt damp as though moisture had been trapped there.

Above her head the light fitting hung forlornly, swaying slightly. The agent had promised to check all the bulbs but he'd forgotten to put one here. She suspected no one had lived here for a long time. It felt so neglected, despite the coat of white emulsion that tried to brighten the walls. It felt, she had to admit, unwelcoming.

Fighting off a feeling of disappointment, she entered the kitchen and pushed the windows open. As she breathed the fresh air her spirits lifted. The noise from the street below was reassuringly normal: traffic, voices, even the faint hum of the sea, just visible beyond the promenade at the end of the street. She filled the kettle and started to open all the cupboards. Apart from a few teabags and a tin of powdered milk, they were all empty but at least they were clean.

She poured boiling water on to a teabag and decided against the powdered milk. She sat down at the Formica-topped table and started to make a shopping list. She was looking forward to doing her own shopping, looking forward to doing all the things she'd never been allowed to do before. She was so engrossed in her own thoughts that she didn't hear a door opening further down the corridor. She was startled as a voice called out, 'Grace, is that you?'

Sam froze, her mug of tea halfway to her lips. There was no time to panic. She forced herself to get up and look out into the gloomy corridor. The door to the small bedroom had swung open and she could hear it creaking eerily as it swayed back and forth.

'Who's there?' she called out, more bravely than she felt. There was an awful moment when all she could see was the shadows rearranging themselves at the end of the corridor. Then a footstep sounded on bare floorboards and something slowly emerged from the doorway.

2

Sam's eyes struggled to make sense of the figure that was coming down the corridor towards her. It was so misshapen it seemed barely human. She tried to speak but her voice refused to come out. Her throat felt as dry as dust. It seemed to take an eternity for the figure to cross the few feet that separated them.

'I knew you'd come,' the voice said. It spoke in a whisper so Sam wasn't even sure she'd heard it correctly.

'Who are you?' she managed to ask. Her own voice sounded as strange as the other's. She felt as if they were both trapped in some awful dream.

'Grace,' the voice exclaimed. Suddenly it was rushing towards her and Sam realized it was only an old woman, half hidden behind an armful of clothes.

Instinctively, Sam held out her hand, whether in defence or welcome she wasn't sure. The old lady faltered. She stood, trembling, and stared at Sam.

'I'm the new tenant. Samantha O'Connor.' She waited for a reply but the old woman remained speechless. She seemed so frail that Sam was ashamed of her earlier fears.

'Are you OK? Let me help you.' She tried to take some of the clothes but the old woman clung to them and refused to let go.

'She does come, you know. Listen, that's her.' Sam jumped as the door swung closed and the corridor was left in darkness again. She felt an icy shiver run down her spine. 'I'll always be here for her. She can count on me.'

'Grace? She's here? Look, why don't you sit down, I'll go and get her.' She led the old woman to a chair and managed to take the pile of dresses from her. They must have been in some cupboard for ages because a strong scent of lavender mingled with mothballs filled her nostrils. 'You wait here,' she said.

As she went into the corridor she could hear the old woman humming a tune as if she'd forgotten about her already. You could tell the corridor never got any sun because the further she went the more cold and damp it felt. When she reached the spare room the door handle felt icy to her touch. She drew back, hesitated, then decided to knock. Nothing. She stood listening. Slowly the truth dawned on her. Even before she opened the door, she knew there was no one there.

She had forgotten how small this room was; it seemed disproportionate to the rest of the flat. Sam could see it was just an ordinary room, but she still had to fight off an urge to walk straight out. There was something claustrophobic about it. Maybe it was the large spider's web that hung from the ceiling. Maybe it was the shutters across the window, which cast a gloomy grey light over everything. She unlatched the catch and pulled them back. One of them hung loosely from its hinge, the peeling paint highlighted by the autumn sunshine. She realized there was dust everywhere. There was a thick layer of it on the window panes and on the floor, now even on her own fingers. The air was full of it. It wasn't even fresh dust. It smelt revoltingly stale and musty. She tried to open the window but it was stuck fast. The frame had begun to rot and she feared the whole thing might drop out down onto the street three storeys below if she persevered.

She wondered why no one had bothered to paint this room too. The flowery wallpaper looked at least fifty years old. Apart from a few rectangles where pictures had once hung, it was so faded she could barely make out the pattern or colours. There was a bit by the door where it had been torn away leaving the plaster exposed. It was like a room time had forgotten. There was absolutely nothing in it other than dust and a few bits of old paper on the floor. She shuddered and hurried out. There was still the problem of the old lady.

'You didn't find her,' the old woman said sadly. She fingered one of the dresses which she held in her lap. It had a pattern of pink roses, not unlike the wallpaper in that room.

'No, I'm sorry. Look, can I get someone for you?'

Suddenly the old lady smiled. 'She'll like you all right. I'm glad you're here. Keep her company.'

'Grace?' Sam asked.

'My little sister. Only seventeen you see. Too young.'

'Yes, of course,' Sam mumbled. She was beginning to feel confused herself. She was relieved when she heard a man's voice shouting up the stairs. She rushed out and leaned over the banister. 'Up here,' she shouted. 'She's up here.'

A lurcher dog bounded up the stairs, followed by its owner. They were both equally thin and shaggy, only the stranger's hair was bleached blond while the dog was an indiscriminate shade of dirty beige. He grabbed the dog by the scruff of its neck and held it back as it tried to jump all over Sam.

'She's up here?' he laughed.

'She seems a bit confused,' Sam told him as she took him through to the kitchen.

'Ben,' the old lady said. 'What are you doing here?'

'What am I doing here? How did you get up all those stairs?'

'I thought I heard Grace,' she told him sadly.

'But Grace isn't here any more, remember,' he said brusquely. 'You know what'll happen if you keep going on about her.'

'Does she live here?' Sam asked.

'Live here? She owns the place. She's lived here all her life. Won't leave, no matter what the family say. Never does what she's told, just like me.'

5

He sounded proud of her. 'Come on, let's get going. I've come for my bath.'

The old woman slowly got to her feet. She held out a frail, bony hand and grabbed Sam's sleeve. 'You will tell me when she comes, won't you? I'm on the ground floor.'

'Don't worry,' Sam reassured her, trying in vain to catch Ben's eye. 'Where is Gr—' she started to ask, but he gave her a warning look. He seemed impatient of their slow progress. The dog had bounded down the corridor and was scratching at the boxroom door.

'Hobo,' he shouted crossly. 'Get away from there.'

The lurcher came towards them unwillingly. He kept looking back and growling. Ben grabbed him by the scruff of the neck and hurried towards the front door, leaving Sam to help the old woman.

When they'd gone Sam realized they'd left the dresses behind. She picked them up and carried them into the living room. It didn't feel like her own home any more. She still didn't know who Grace was, but she couldn't shake off the feeling that she was a presence in the flat.

3

That first night Sam was too excited to sleep. She lay in bed reliving the day's events; seeing again the anxious expression on her parents' faces as the train pulled out of the station. They didn't understand why she'd had to get away. Her sister Kate was the only one who'd encouraged her. If it hadn't been for Kate she'd never have survived the past two years; the succession of doctors and therapists, the well-intentioned visitors who always had some new solution to her 'problem'.

She looked at the clock. Midnight. She could hear someone crying in the flat below, a soft muffled sound that was impossible to ignore. She got up and went to the window. She could just see the traffic moving along the seafront and, beyond it, the dark mass of the sea. It was Saturday night and there were still a lot of people about. On impulse she decided to go out and join them. Why not? There was no one to stop her.

She dressed quickly and went out, creeping down the stairs as silently as she could. She pulled the hood up on her jacket and walked briskly down to the seafront. The tide was low but the wind had whipped the surface of the water into a myriad whitecaps. Almost directly in front of her the ruined West Pier glimmered mysteriously in the moonlight. By some trick of the wind, music seemed to drift from its empty rooms as if the night had somehow restored it to life. Around its legs dark pools reflected shadows which seemed to move with a life of their own. Then she realized there was someone there. Someone was moving under the pier. Whoever it was lit a cigarette and the sudden flare of light sent the shadows fleeing.

She heard a dog bark somewhere below her and the sound of feet running across the stony beach. A figure emerged from the shadow of the pier and joined the newcomers. Sam could hear shouting and laughter as they jostled and pushed each other into the shallows. She drew back as someone's eyes unexpectedly met hers. Suddenly she felt alone and vulnerable. She realized the traffic had stopped. Behind her the hotels were all in darkness. She'd been standing here for ages and was chilled to the bone.

Back in the flat, she climbed into the high bed and pulled the duvet over her head. She soon fell into a restless, disturbed sleep. She woke in the night not knowing where she was. The ceilings were so much higher than in her bedroom at home. Light streamed in from the streetlight outside, making the shadows so much denser. Through the open door, the corridor seemed packed tight with darkness. Directly opposite was the door to the boxroom. She could hear the window shuddering in its frame each time a lone car sped down the street.

There were other strange noises too. The bedsprings creaked when she turned over and somewhere in the empty rooms she could hear floorboards settling as if unseen feet had just passed over them. Occasionally, too, there was movement downstairs as if someone else couldn't sleep. The noises seeped into her dreams until she wasn't sure if she was awake or dreaming. Once, when she opened her eyes to look at the clock, she thought she saw someone standing in the doorway, watching her. She blinked and it was gone. Only a shadow, she thought, as she drifted back into sleep.

4

The next morning Sam washed and dressed quickly before hurrying out. It was a bright September morning and the seafront was busy. Yet even in this sunshine the old pier looked dark and mysterious. It seemed so decrepit she wondered how it had survived so long. The tide was high and waves were breaking against the metal framework which held up the deck. Even at this distance, she could see it was corroded and orange with rust. It looked as though it could collapse at any minute, spilling buildings, railings, and little pagodas down into the waiting sea.

Despite the bright sunshine, Sam shivered. She went down to the lower promenade and walked over the narrow strip of beach to the water's edge. The water looked brown and murky, with dark clumps of seaweed swirling around in the current. The waves broke noisily a few inches from where she stood. They sucked hungrily at the pebbles before spewing them back again. She could feel the spray on her face, as if the sea was just waiting to draw her into its current too. For the first time in her life, no one was telling her to be careful. She edged closer to the water, letting the waves creep round her trainers, feeling the pebbles slide under her feet as the beach gave way to the pull of the current.

Sam's legs were shaking as she walked back to the promenade. She sat just beyond the shadow of the old pier and dialled home.

'Hello, Dad, it's me,' she said brightly.

'Samantha, everything OK?' he asked. She could hear her mum say something in the background, imagine her rushing over to take the phone, her face intense and worried, a hundred questions she wanted to ask.

'I'm fine,' she told him, 'really enjoying myself.'

'You've got everything you need?' Her mother had managed to get the phone now. 'You're sure you've got enough food for the weekend? I wish you'd let us drive you down. We could have done all your shopping.'

'Mum. Let's not go over that again. I want to look after myself, you know that. I went shopping yesterday as soon as I arrived. And the shops are open all the time here anyway. Yes, I can carry everything. It's no problem, really. Look, I said I'm fine. The flat's fine. The weather's fine. Everything's fine. Happy?' Why did her mother always make her so cross? Why couldn't she understand that she needed to be independent?

'I just want to be sure that you're safe. It's natural to worry,' her mother said defensively. 'It is the first time you've been away from home.'

9

Left home, Sam corrected her silently.

'Just don't overdo it. You know what the doctor said.'

'He said I should get a life, remember. I can look after myself. You have to trust me. Look, put Dad back on again,' Sam said crossly.

She only half listened to her dad tell her all about the new plants he'd bought for the garden. She was looking out to sea, watching the windsurfers circling around. Suddenly a lone cloud blocked the sun, causing Sam to look up at the sky. As her gaze passed over the old pier an unexpected patch of colour caught her eye. With a start she realized there was someone there; a woman in a summer dress, its colours like a bright stain against the white railing. She was leaning over the edge, staring down at the water as it swirled round the pier legs. Sam worried the rail might not hold. How did she get up there? The pier ended about thirty feet from the shore and the only access was via a narrow walkway that was blocked by a huge security gate surrounded by barbed wire. For a horrible moment Sam thought she was going to jump. Her father's voice broke into her thoughts.

'Sam, Sam, are you all right?'

'Sorry, Dad. I just saw someone. I . . . ' Sam stared, blinked, looked again. There was no doubt about it, the woman was gone. She scanned the water, searching for and dreading a patch of bright colour in the dark water that swirled beneath the pier. 'I thought I saw someone, but it's nothing. Just a reflection, I suppose.'

'You had me worried there. You take care of yourself. Don't forget to keep in touch. You know how your mother worries.'

'Yes, Dad. I will. I promise. Tell Kate to ring later. Enjoy your lunch.'

Sam put the phone back in her bag and looked around. The beach was beginning to fill up. A few hardy families had decided to brave the September wind and had set up their deckchairs and windscreens. In front of her a man was struggling with the Sunday papers while his kids hurled pebbles at each other. She could hear the music drifting over from the bars further down the beach. It was all reassuringly normal. So why couldn't she shake off the feeling she'd witnessed something strange? The sun had come out again and everything was bathed in a bright clear light, but nowhere was there any sign of a woman in a summer dress.

5

The next few days were so busy that Sam felt she was living a double life. Her days were filled with excitement, discovering new places to go, making plans for the future, adding some personal touches to the flat to make it feel more like her own space. She bought a poster for the living room wall, a couple of embroidered Indian cushions for the sofa, some brightly coloured mugs for the kitchen.

During the hours of daylight she revelled in her new life, but after dark the doubts began to creep in. No matter how tired she felt when she went to bed she found it difficult to get to sleep. The flat seemed to change, to revert to some strange life of its own. It was nothing specific. Nothing, she knew, other than her own imagination magnifying each slight sound into something it couldn't possibly be. Footsteps walking up the corridor, doors opening and closing. Even the feeling that someone was there, waiting just behind her bedroom door.

The persistent noise from the flat below didn't help. How could she sleep once that crying started? It was so mournful it seemed to fill her mind with terrible images making the future look dark and hopeless. She hadn't met the occupants yet and wasn't sure that she wanted to. They must be out all day because she never heard a thing until late at night. Sometimes it seemed as if they only came to life when she began to drift off to sleep.

She began to dread the moment when she had to switch off the lights and walk down that long gloomy corridor to her bedroom. The doors worried her, whether they were open or closed, whether she could see the shadows lurking there or only imagine them. By the end of the first week she was so tired that her nervousness began to spill over into the hours of daylight. By Friday evening she was exhausted. Sam settled herself on the sofa and tried to relax. She found a station playing music she liked on the radio and turned the volume up. It felt like her space now. The music banished all those strange noises and filled her with energy. Yet her eyes felt heavy. She could hardly keep them open.

Some hours later she woke with a start, convinced that someone had just whispered something in her ear. It was pitch dark. She looked around in confusion. She switched the lamp on, but its light seemed dull and distant as if the air in the room could not sustain it. She had a strange sensation that she was trapped in some half world between sleep and waking, where anything might happen. No, she was too sleepy to be properly awake.

Her eyes had started to close again when she heard it for a second time. Someone was whispering, but like a bad connection on the phone, she couldn't make out what they were saying. For a moment she even imagined she could feel cold breath on her skin. She tried to ignore it and drift back to sleep, but it was impossible. The room was freezing cold. She felt as if icy fingers had touched every bone in her body, making it impossible for her to move. She thought of those bodies, trapped in ice, that lay undisturbed for hundreds of years while life went on all around them. Travellers who'd paused to rest and fallen asleep never to wake. Had she been dreaming of ice?

A sudden burst of static forced her wide awake and she realized she'd left the radio on. It must be later than she thought. The station had closed for the night, but occasionally it was picking up fragments of more distant transmissions. It sounded as if some unseen hand was continually turning the dial, searching for something they couldn't find. All the voices were so disjointed they became meaningless noise. That was why Sam was so shocked when the interference fell away and suddenly there was someone talking as clearly as if they were sitting right next to her.

'Next Sunday, Harry Pearson and his orchestra. Tickets one shilling.'

Another burst of static made it impossible to hear more. She stretched across to turn it off but the switch seemed to be jammed. The static intensified. She couldn't shake off the conviction that some voice was trying to get through, that if she listened intently enough she would finally get the message.

Sam got up wearily and switched the radio off at the socket. The room was plunged into darkness. There was a last burst of static, then silence. Sam fumbled at the socket, trying to plug the lamp back in. She felt someone was watching her, willing her to fail. Her hand felt clumsy and uncoordinated. She was so tired she couldn't think straight. Her mind was still functioning in dream logic. After a few seconds the light came back on and her eye suddenly caught the pile of old dresses still heaped on the armchair. There must be a draught from the corridor because the fabric was fluttering slightly. She stared as the pattern of pink roses and big yellow daisies swelled and fell. She even imagined she could smell roses. The colours seemed so bright, not faded at all.

As she watched, the dress slid down to the floor as if in slow motion. For a moment it hung in the air, the skirts billowing in some ghostly breeze from a summer long gone. Then it collapsed in a heap on the carpet. Sam stopped to pick it up on her way to bed. It was just an old dress, the cotton worn and limp in her hands. She put it back on the chair. She must remember to take the whole lot down to the old lady tomorrow. She switched off the lamp and opened the door into the corridor, prepared to brave the few seconds of darkness before her hand found the light switch. Only it wasn't dark. There was a faint but unmistakable light coming from the spare room.

6

As Sam walked slowly down the corridor the light seemed to waver as if about to be extinguished at any minute. She felt strangely detached. She no longer felt cold or even frightened. She wasn't feeling anything at all, except a mild surprise, when she arrived at the boxroom door and saw it was wedged open. The only light in the room came from the streetlight outside. The wind had grown stronger and the light was tossed and tangled in the branches of a roadside tree. For some reason it reminded Sam of the bottom of the sea. She moved through it slowly, as though wading through deep water, and closed the shutters. Immediately the light fell into a few narrow strips on the dusty floor.

Sam pulled the wedge of paper from under the door and tossed it into the room, closing the door behind her. Her bedroom clock told her it was 4.20 a.m. She was so tired she was almost asleep on her feet. Without bothering to undress she climbed into the high bed and fell into a deep sleep as soon as her head touched the pillow.

Outside, clouds raced across the night sky. The windows rattled in their frames as the wind roared up from the sea and battered the buildings. In the boxroom the shutter fell open, swinging against the wall with a dull, regular thud. Sam heard it in her dreams. She was walking on the pier. It was high tide and waves came crashing over the railing, breaking around her feet. Strings of lights swayed above her, suspended from the ornate ironwork where giant fish curled their tails and flapped metal fins. She could hear music coming from the concert hall at the end of the pier, but however far she walked it never seemed any closer. When she looked down she saw the decking was worn and rotting, leaving great gaps where the ocean surged through. She realized her skirts were soaked and heavy, like a weight dragging her down towards the cold salty water.

It was still dark when she was awoken by the sound of a door banging. She glanced at the clock. 5.00 a.m. She'd barely slept at all. She tried to ignore the noise and sink straight back into sleep, but it was too loud. The room felt cold and damp. She could hear the sea, imagine the waves breaking angrily on the shingle. It sounded so close. She pulled the duvet over her head and tried to block everything out, but it was impossible. She didn't want to get up. She definitely didn't want to face the long, gloomy corridor, but she couldn't ignore the constant banging. Reluctantly, she sat up and looked around the shadowy room, gradually reassuring herself that the dark shapes were only the old-fashioned wardrobe and chest of drawers. Only then did she switch on the light and get out of bed.

She crossed the room quickly and opened her bedroom door. In front of her the door to the spare room was wide open, swaying slightly as if moved by some unseen force.

The light from her bedroom fell into the room in a wide strip, leaving the edges packed with dense shadow. She went to switch on the light and was startled when her fingers touched a damp patch on the wall. Suddenly the door swung towards her, catching her painfully on the shoulder. She tried to push it away but it felt as if someone was pushing it from the other side. She pushed harder and this time the door gave way so easily that she fell into the room and landed awkwardly on her knees. By her hand was the wedge of paper that had jammed the door. It seemed to be part of an old programme for a concert on the pier.

Sam looked at it disbelievingly, hearing again the music from her dream. Only she knew she wasn't dreaming now. Under the harsh light of the bare bulb the room was squalid and depressing. The air was so damp and fetid that it was hard to breathe. A feeling of revulsion swept over her. She scrambled to her feet and closed the door, making sure she'd turned the handle fully so it wouldn't blow open again. But even back in bed, she couldn't get warm and she lay shivering until the dawn finally broke and the plaintive cry of the gulls assured her that the day had really begun.

7

When Sam eventually got up it was almost lunch time. The wind had dropped and the sun was shining. She noticed the door to the spare room had blown open again. Rain must have seeped in through the rotting window frame because there was a small pool of water on the floor. The shutter was hanging at an odd angle and Sam went in to try and fix it, but discovered that the hinge had snapped. The wind had done nothing to clear the air in the room; it was still stale only now the whole room smelt damp too. The strong sunlight made everything look worse, showing up the grime that streaked the windows and the dust that coated the floor. As she stared at it she began to notice strange patterns in the dust, as if something had been dragged across the floor.

In the corner, where she had thrown it, was the wedge of paper that had held open the door. With a jolt, she realized the events of the night before had really happened. They hadn't been just a dream. She felt a strange reluctance to touch it, but she forced herself to pick it up. She stared at it in disbelief. It was just a bit of white card. There was no writing on it at all. Had she imagined it? She didn't want to even think about that possibility. Later. She'd come in later and clean the whole room, have another go at opening the window, let in some fresh air, get rid of that awful smell.

She hurried up the corridor. She was relieved to arrive in the big, sunny living room, as though she had crossed an invisible frontier between two worlds. But this morning the air wasn't that fresh here either. As she went to open the window she realized it was the pile of old dresses giving off their musty smell of mothballs and lavender. Why had she left them there so long? She'd take them down to the old lady as soon as she'd had a cup of coffee.

As Sam walked down the three flights of stairs the house seemed very quiet. She hadn't met any of the other tenants yet. There was only one flat on each floor, so there couldn't be many people living here, but it did seem strange that she'd never even caught a glimpse of anyone. It made her feel more alone than she really was. She stopped to rearrange the dresses which were slipping out of her grasp. For a second she had the sense that someone was watching her. She looked up the wide stairwell half expecting to see a face looking down at her, but there was nothing but shadows.

The old lady's door had a panel of engraved glass with a pattern of birds and flowers. Sam knocked loudly in case she couldn't hear very well. It was opened immediately by a strange man, who stood scowling at her. She took a step back in surprise.

'Yes?' he said abruptly.

'I'm from upstairs. The top floor. I've brought the dresses back.' She wondered why he was still looking at her so oddly. She could swear she'd seen him shudder. 'They were left in my flat. Your . . . your . . . ' Sam stopped. 'Who are you?' she asked. 'I'm afraid I don't know anyone's name yet, apart from Ben.'

'Oh, you're a friend of his, are you? You don't look like one of his lot. You'd better come in. Jonathon Stacy. Mrs Armstrong is my aunt by marriage.'

He walked away without offering to help her.

'I'm not really a friend. I mean, I just met him last week,' Sam said to his back. 'I found Mrs Armstrong in my flat. He came to help,' she finished awkwardly.

'Came to scrounge money, more likely,' he said with a sneer as he led her into the front room. 'A visitor for you, aunt,' he announced. 'She didn't introduce herself, but she claims she's the new tenant. Says she's a friend of Ben's.' He had raised his voice and Sam saw his aunt flinch.

'I'm not deaf yet,' she said crossly.

'Hello, Mrs Armstrong. Do you remember me? I'm Sam O'Connor. I moved in last week.'

'Of course I remember,' she said, looking from Sam's face to the pile of dresses in her arms. A smile broke over her face. 'So Grace did come. I told you she would.'

'Now, Auntie,' her nephew butted in, 'we'll have no more of that. You know Grace is dead. She died before I was born. Well I never,' he said, turning round in surprise as Sam's arms suddenly gave way and all the dresses dropped to the floor.

8

Sam felt such a fool. 'I don't know what came over me,' she said as she helped Jonathon pick up the dresses.

'Here,' Jonathon said brusquely, 'you'd better sit down. I'll get rid of these.'

'Put the kettle on while you're at it,' the old lady commanded. As soon as he had left the room Mrs Armstrong winked at Sam and said, 'They're all after my money, you know. That's the only reason they come to visit.' She made no attempt to lower her voice. 'All apart from Ben, that is. You'll like him. Money means nothing to him.'

'He's a disgrace,' Jonathon said as he came back into the room with a tray of cups and saucers. 'The family should disown him. I don't know what my cousin Hope was thinking of, going off to Greece and leaving him to run wild like that.' He stopped suddenly as if embarrassed he had said too much. He started to shove the dresses into a black bin bag. Mrs Armstrong watched him disapprovingly but didn't say anything.

'Where is Ben?' Sam asked, trying to sound indifferent.

'Where? You tell me. Lives like a gypsy. No respect for his family.' Jonathon tied the top of the bin bag and chucked it into the corridor.

'You're not to throw them out,' the old lady ordered.

'Did I say I was going to do that? I'll stick them in the cellar later. They'll be perfectly all right.' He poured out the tea and handed the cups around.

'You forgot the biscuits, Jonathon,' Mrs Armstrong said crossly. 'You know we always have chocolate biscuits when we have visitors. Always interfering,' she said as he left the room. 'No wonder his wife left him.'

Sam felt awkward. Her family wasn't anything like this. 'Tell me about the dresses,' she said, eager to change the subject.

The old lady's mood changed instantly. 'Beautiful, aren't they?' she smiled. 'Nothing but the best for Grace. She was quite a beauty, you know. Had all the boys after her.' Mrs Armstrong shook her head as if the memories were too strong for her frail body. 'Even after . . . well, I mustn't bore you. An old woman has nothing but memories. They get more vivid every day. It's a terrible thing, old age.' She raised her voice suddenly as Jonathon returned to the room carrying a plate of biscuits. 'You're at the mercy of your relatives,' she said, staring straight at him.

'You know what happens if you upset yourself, Auntie. She mustn't overdo it,' Jonathon addressed Sam.

Sam wanted to ask what had happened to Grace but it seemed impossible with Jonathon in the room. She finished her tea and got up to leave. Mrs Armstrong was nodding off in her seat, her chocolate biscuit melting in her hand. Jonathon made no attempt to take the biscuit away. Instead, he followed Sam to the door and said, 'We try not to mention Grace. It just upsets her. She gets confused. She should be in a home.' He paused and stared at her for a moment. 'Look, here's my card. Keep an eye on her, will you? Let me know if anything happens. It'd be for her own good, of course. I'm only thinking of her,' he said defensively.

Sam looked down at the card he had given her. It said Jonathon Stacy, Solicitor, and gave an address in Eastbourne. 'I'll visit her another day,' she said. But I'm not going to spy on her, she added under her breath. She was relieved when the flat door closed. What had he meant about not asking about her sister? Was there some family secret she wasn't supposed to know? But Grace had been dead for ages, nothing she'd done could matter now.

It was easy to forget about Grace during the day. But after dark, lying in bed all alone in the large flat, she couldn't get her out of her mind. She snuggled into the duvet, trying to keep the cold draught off her face. Downstairs someone was restless too. As usual Sam could hear their footsteps pacing up and down the corridor. The footsteps crossed over into her dreams. Only now they were dancing and they belonged to Grace.

9

On Monday afternoon Sam walked into the town centre and registered at an employment agency. There was plenty of work cleaning, but not much else. With no experience, an adviser told her, her options were limited. Nevertheless, Sam was sure she'd find something. She had enough money for the next three or four weeks so there was no need to take the first job she was offered.

Her doctor had advised her to get plenty of exercise so she decided to walk home along the seafront. The wind was much stronger here making her skin tingle and her eyes water. The tide was coming in and there were huge waves as far as the eye could see. The sound of them crashing on the pebbled beach filled the air and shut out the noise of the traffic behind her. In the distance she could see the old pier, looking even more sad and abandoned as the waves broke against its rusting framework and threatened to overwhelm it. She tried to imagine the empty rooms filled with people having fun, children playing on the decking, the sun sparkling on the water, but couldn't do it.

Yet as she got nearer she could hear music coming from the deserted buildings. It sounded like the beat of a drum. She thought it must be the sound of the sea echoing through the empty rooms but as she got closer she saw it was drums. A small group of young people were gathered under a remnant of the pier, playing an assortment of drums of all shapes and sizes. The boys all had long, unwashed hair while some of the girls had shaved heads and elaborate tattoos. They were dressed in scruffy, tribal clothes. On the outskirts of their circle two dogs were fighting half heartedly. Sam realized one of them was Hobo and looking around noticed Ben sitting on the wall. He signalled to her to join him.

'Hi,' she said shyly. Hobo bounded over to greet her, looking even more dishevelled than she'd remembered. She patted him gingerly, wondering when he ever got a bath. There were half a dozen other dogs too, some with scarves tied cowboy style round their necks. 'I met your Uncle Jonathon the other day,' she told him. 'I don't think he likes me.'

'Join the club,' he smiled. 'He doesn't care about anything except money. My grandfather left him a share in the house, but he can't touch it while Gran's alive. He wants to put her in a home. He's not really my uncle. He's my mother's cousin.'

'Families,' Sam sighed.

Ben turned to look at her. 'So tell me about yours.'

'Oh, there's just me and my sister, Kate. She's a handful, always in trouble, but always gets away with it.' She didn't want to talk about herself, not yet. There was an awkward pause while she struggled with memories of her illness. She wanted to forget, to put it all behind her, but that wasn't so easy.

Ben watched her. The wind had blown her hair loose from the slide that had held it and it fanned around her head like a dark halo. 'We all have our reasons for leaving home.

Maxine was in care. She's been living rough since she was thirteen.' He pointed to a tall, painfully thin girl who was dancing, eyes closed, to the beat of the drums. She was dressed all in black apart from the Indian bracelets that jangled on both wrists. 'Andy's on the run, Billy's dad used to beat him, and Jade, over there, they tried to lock her up in a psychiatric ward.'

Sam stared at Jade. She looked like a warrior princess from a science fiction movie. She had long black hair that was twisted into dreadlocks and piled up haphazardly on top of her head. She wore a necklace of crystals strung on a leather thong, loose printed trousers, and a thin summer vest. She seemed unaware of the cold wind.

'They're my family now. We support each other,' Ben told her.

'Where do you live?' Sam asked.

'Here.' He gestured around him.

'Here? In Brighton?'

'Yes, here,' he said, enjoying her surprise. 'We've squatted the beach huts. They won't bother us until the season starts again, and we'll have moved on before then. It's a mistake to stay anywhere too long.'

They walked across to the remains of an old walled garden where a bonfire was burning. The driftwood hissed and crackled as the flames curled around it, sending off a thick cloud of pungent smoke. 'The kitchen. All mod cons,' Ben said, pointing to a blackened kettle that was balanced precariously on the burning wood. 'Spacious living room, splendid view.'

Sam laughed. 'I've got a spacious living room,' she said. 'In fact, I think I've got a bit too much space.'

'You're settling in OK though? There isn't anything wrong, is there?'

'No, why should there be?' Ben avoided her eye. 'What is it? Is there something I should know?'

'It's nothing,' Ben said. 'It's just that flat's been empty for ages. Gran always refused to rent it before. I don't know what Jonathon said to make her change her mind.'

'It does feel a bit strange at night,' Sam admitted, thinking of the long gloomy corridor. 'I suppose I'm not used to being alone, or to such old houses. And I haven't met any of the neighbours yet.'

'Don't get your hopes up. The family on the first floor don't even speak to my gran.'

'What about downstairs? Who lives there?' Sam asked, hoping it might be somebody young.

'That's Hope's flat.'

'Hope?'

'My mother, she's got the flat below yours. She's OK. You'll like her, if you stick it out until the spring.'

'What do you mean?' Sam asked.

'She never winters here. Can't stand the cold. She has a house in Greece. Rents it out in the summer, then moves in herself once the season finishes. It's . . . Sam, what is it?'

'You're sure the flat's empty?' Sam felt a shiver run down her spine, stealing all the heat from her body. 'There couldn't be somebody staying there?'

'Of course I'm sure. I've got a spare key if you don't believe me. Hey, don't look so sad. You'll meet people soon.' Ben smiled encouragingly.

'It's not that,' Sam said quickly. 'I like living on my own.'

'Then what is it? I know something's wrong. You've gone as white as a ghost.'

'It's nothing.' She hesitated. 'It's just I was sure I heard someone moving around down there.' She decided not to mention her strange experience on Friday night.

'It's probably the central heating. Always was noisy.'

'Yes,' Sam agreed, 'the heating is a bit ancient. It gets really cold at night.' She stopped suddenly, realizing it must be much colder in the beach huts. 'But I heard doors opening and closing too. I sound crazy, don't I?' She gave a half-hearted laugh. After all, it was a very old house. The sounds could have come from anywhere, those footsteps, the voices. They couldn't have been from the floor below.

'I wouldn't live there,' Ben said, throwing a stick for Hobo. 'Not on my own.'

'Thanks. Now I feel much better.'

'Hey, just joking. You should talk to Jade, she's always seeing ghosts.'

'Who said anything about ghosts?'

'Footsteps in an empty flat. Sounds like a ghost to me.'

'Maybe it's Grace. Your gran's convinced she comes back.' Sam laughed.

Ben tensed. 'Forget about Grace,' he said crossly. 'Just forget all about her.'

10

The following day Sam was just on her way out when her mobile began to ring. 'Hello? It's you, Kate. At last, I thought you'd forgotten me.'

'Your phone was switched off,' Kate grumbled. 'Anyway, you could have rung me. So how is it?'

'You'll have to come and see for yourself. Just don't bring Mum and Dad yet. I don't want them trying to organize everything.'

'As if I would,' Kate said indignantly. 'Really, you know I can't wait to get away. I've got a new outfit I'm dying to wear, but I can't wear it here.'

'Well, if that's the only reason you want to come,' she said, wondering if she was really ready for the responsibility of looking after Kate for a whole weekend.

'I'm so bored. Nothing exciting ever happens here,' Kate moaned. 'So tell me everything.'

'I've only been here a week,' Sam laughed, 'but quite a lot has happened. I've met the old lady who owns the house, and her grandson, Ben.'

'Go on, tell me about Ben.'

'He's squatting down by the beach. He lives with all these strange people, and his dog.'

'And . . . ' Kate interrupted.

'And I've only just met him, but he is cute.'

'You see, I was right. You can't hide anything from me.'

'There isn't anything to hide. I'm not sure he even likes me,' she said, thinking of his sudden change of mood when she'd made a joke about Grace.

'It's not fair. Why should you get all the excitement?' Kate moaned. 'I'm stuck here where nothing ever happens.'

'That's because you're only thirteen. And anyway, I think you've had a more exciting life than me,' Sam said reproachfully.

'I'm sorry, I wasn't thinking. You know I didn't mean it like that. But you've no idea what it's been like since you left. They're on at me all the time. Where are you going? Who are you meeting? Be home by ten. You needn't think you're going out in that skirt. It's non-stop.'

Sam had to smile. Kate was a good mimic. 'And I'm sure you go ahead and do exactly what you want.'

'Of course! And now I want to come and stay with you. What about next weekend?'

'Well, let me see. I'll just check my busy social calendar. I think I can just squeeze you in.' Sam laughed. 'I don't know why I miss you so much, but I do. Ring again soon, Kate.'

'I will. You are OK, aren't you? You're not feeling ill or anything?' Kate was genuinely concerned.

'No, I'm fine, really. I've never felt better. I know I've done the right thing,' Sam assured her. 'It's just a bit lonely sometimes.'

26

'I could come down tomorrow. Take a few days off school.'

'Certainly not. They'd never let you and Mum would rush down instead. Promise you won't say anything.'

'As if I would. Of course I promise. Look, got to go now. I'll ring soon, bye.'

Just hearing Kate's voice made her feel better. She'd been spending too much time alone, letting her imagination work overtime. She'd have to be more careful. She knew she couldn't afford to take any risks with her health. There was nothing wrong with the flat, at least, nothing worse than a few draughts and a damp patch. As for the boxroom, she knew how to fix that.

She went into the kitchen and began to fill a bucket with soapy water. She was singing along to the radio when she noticed how cold it had become. As she turned off the taps she thought she heard footsteps in the flat below, but remembered that it was empty. Just a noise, she thought uncertainly. Nothing to worry about. She thought of her sister and how different everything would feel with her in the flat. Then she heard it again. It definitely was footsteps, like someone in a high heeled shoe. Only it wasn't downstairs. She put the bucket down and looked out into the corridor. She'd replaced the bulb but it still seemed gloomy and unwelcoming.

'Hello,' she called, not even liking the sound of her own voice breaking the silence. No one replied. 'Mrs Armstrong?' she said, quietly this time. She glanced into the living room and shrugged. There was no one there and she could see the chain was still in place on the front door.

She wished Ben hadn't told her that no one had lived here for ages. She wanted to believe there was nothing strange about the flat, but there had to be some reason it had been left empty so long. Something to do with the old lady and her sister Grace. Not being able to let go, her therapist would call it. Well, Sam had let go of her own past and she wasn't going to let anyone hold her back now. She collected the bucket and walked down to the spare room filled with a new determination. She knew that if she could reclaim that room, the whole flat would seem different. The past would be banished, put back where it belonged.

She was annoyed to see another pool of water on the floor. Where had it come from? It hadn't been raining. She bent down to mop it up and caught sight of herself reflected in its quivering surface. Only somehow it wasn't a self she recognized. It was her face, but it was as if someone else was looking out through her eyes. She mopped it up quickly and wrung out the cloth.

She really needed to open the window and let in some fresh air. She managed to force the catch but however hard she pushed the window wouldn't budge. She left the bucket on the floor while she went to get a chair from the kitchen. As soon as she entered the corridor she noticed how quiet it had become. She realized she couldn't have heard footsteps in this flat because her own feet made no noise at all. The same dull blue carpet was fitted everywhere except the boxroom and the kitchen. Now the silence seemed oppressive so she put on her Walkman and turned the volume up to a satisfying level.

When she got back she was amazed to see the window wide open. There were flakes of white paint on the floor, as if someone had run a knife along the top of the frame. She began to clean the small panes of glass, resisting the temptation to keep looking behind her. She was aware how far it was to the flat door, even further to the street, three storeys below. But at least there was fresh air in the room now and soon, with the window clean, there'd be more light too. What it really needed was a coat of paint and a few pictures on the wall, then the room would be transformed. She could imagine sitting here with Kate, laughing about everything.

Despite all her hard work, it wasn't so easy to wash away

the decades of grime. As the panes dried they looked as dirty as ever. The sun had begun to set and the whole street was in shadow. She had to admit the room looked gloomier than ever. There was no point in continuing now, better to leave the rest until the morning. She forced the window closed and struggled to fasten the catch. As she finally managed to close it the chair tilted unexpectedly and she had to jump clear. The Walkman fell from her pocket and landed with a horrible crunch on the floor. The back sprang open, the batteries flew out and spun noisily on the floorboards. While Sam was picking them up a sudden blast of wind shook the window frame. It rattled so violently she feared it would be forced into the room. Dead leaves from the nearby tree were flung at the glass and seemed to cling there, further blocking the light. The wind howled like an animal in pain. Then, as suddenly as it had begun, it stopped.

There was an unnatural silence, as if all the world outside the room had ceased to exist. Not a single car passed down the street. No voices drifted from any window. Not even a floorboard creaking. As if everything was holding its breath, waiting. Sam couldn't move a muscle. She stayed, hunched down, the batteries in her palm, listening with every fibre of her being. Then it began. The slow drip, drip of water. In front of her eyes the small pool of water began to reform on the floor. A damp, fetid smell filled the air. Sam could barely breathe. She felt all the air was being sucked from the room. Then she heard the door slam shut behind her.

11

Sam's hand couldn't get a grip on the door handle. Its surface was damp and slimy as if it had been immersed in stagnant water. She fought off the feeling of panic that threatened to overwhelm her, grabbed the cloth she'd been using on the window and tried again. It still wouldn't open. The door seemed to have jammed. Had the old lock been accidentally activated when the door slammed shut? She had to keep trying. At last, to her relief, the handle turned. She wrenched the door open and fled up the corridor, gasping at the air as though her lungs would collapse.

When she could breathe again she tried to calm herself. There had to be some rational explanation. A sudden draught might account for the door but what about the water? She knew it hadn't leaked through the ceiling or the window panes. It wasn't raining. It hadn't rained for days. It seemed to just appear out of thin air. And that awful smell. It was so sudden, so overpowering. She hadn't imagined it. There was something in that room. Something that didn't want to be disturbed, didn't want her to let in the fresh air and clean away all the dust and grime. Something, she hated to admit, that didn't want her there at all.

It was nearly seven o'clock. Another hour and it would be dark. She was dreading what might happen then, but there was no way she was going to give in. This was her home now. She'd find out all she could about the flat and what had happened here. And there was only one person who could tell her that.

The stairwell was already dark and full of shadows as she hurried down it. She banged noisily on Mrs Armstrong's door. Through the frosted glass she saw a figure approaching, but it seemed to take an age before the door was edged open.

'Oh, it's you,' Mrs Armstrong said, as she struggled to free the door chain. 'You've come to tell me about Grace.'

'Something's happened. There's . . . there's . . . ' How could she put it all into words? What had really happened and would anyone believe her? Even in the worst days of her illness, she'd never felt as totally alone as this.

'I knew she'd come,' Mrs Armstrong said quietly. 'She won't hurt you, you know. She doesn't mean any harm. Grace was always such a gentle creature.'

'You must tell me everything,' Sam demanded. 'What happened in that room?'

She followed the old lady into the living room and waited while she settled herself in her chair. Her head was filled with so many questions she barely knew where to begin.

Mrs Armstrong lowered her voice to a whisper. 'You mustn't tell anyone. They don't understand. They want to sell the house, you know, and I can't have that. This is her home. It'll always be her home, as long as I live. I promised her that.'

'You lived in my flat?'

'Yes, we lived in the whole house in those days. The top floor was the nursery. We both slept up there with the nanny.'

'So my spare room . . . ?'

'When nanny left Grace moved into that room. She was so pleased to have a room of her own. She chose the paper herself. She loved flowers, especially roses.' She paused to wipe her eyes, then continued. 'I don't blame her. It wasn't her fault.'

'Of course it wasn't,' Sam said gently, feeling more confused than ever. 'You must have loved her very much.'

'Yes, she was my little sister. I always felt responsible for her. You see, father died when we were both still children, mother was so strict, and Grace was always too sensitive for her own good.'

31

'What happened to her?' Sam asked. For some reason she was feeling calmer already.

'Such a tragic life. I can't forgive myself.' Mrs Armstrong's hand shook as she picked up her handbag and began to rummage inside. 'Here,' she said, passing Sam a photo.

It was much smaller than a modern photo. The paper was quite creased, as if it had been handled too much. Grace was standing next to a young man in uniform. She was wearing the rose-patterned dress Sam had found in her flat, with a corsage of silk flowers pinned at the waist. Her long golden hair was blowing in the wind and she held it back from her face with a tiny, gloved hand. The couple were standing on the promenade, with the West Pier in the background. Their arms were linked and they were smiling lovingly at each other. Their faces were so young Sam was reminded of children playing grown-ups.

'That was taken the day they announced their engagement,' Mrs Armstrong said, putting the photo back in her bag. 'He'd been away for a year, you see. Came back on leave and asked her to marry him. She was too young of course, only sixteen. Mother wanted them to wait, but it was the war. No one wanted to wait for anything. Afterwards mother kept saying they should have listened to her; she knew all along it was a bad idea. But it wouldn't have made any difference.' The old lady's voice faltered.

'But what did happen?' Sam asked firmly, determined not to be put off. 'I have to know.'

'Why, he died of course. Poor Bob, such a bright young man. Had a place at medical school, but he signed up instead. They all did. Men were proud to serve their country in those days. He fought in the Battle of Britain. His plane didn't come back one day. No one saw him go down so he was reported as lost at sea.' Mrs Armstrong stopped speaking. Sam wondered if she should leave her alone with her memories, but she hadn't found out everything she needed to know yet. It would be dark soon and she'd have to face another night in the flat alone.

'Did Grace die there?' she asked softly.

Mrs Armstrong couldn't speak. She nodded her head feebly and clutched at her hanky. 'She never got over it. Locked herself in; had his photos all over the room. She just seemed to waste away.' The old lady's face crumpled and she began to cry. 'You must think I'm a foolish old woman,' she managed at last, 'but it seems like it happened yesterday to me.'

'No, I don't,' Sam assured her. 'I've got a younger sister too. I'm sorry, but I have to ask. How do you know she comes? Have you seen her?'

'No, dear. She doesn't show herself to me, but I knew she'd like you.'

'What does she want?' Sam asked anxiously, thinking of the strange footsteps she'd heard in the corridor.

Mrs Armstrong looked shocked. 'This is her home. Where else would she go?'

12

Sam felt calmer but even more confused as she climbed the stairs back to her flat. She felt sorry for Mrs Armstrong, but she mustn't accept everything she'd said. She wasn't ready to believe that Grace was a real presence in the house. After all, no one had seen her. She wasn't sure what she believed. She knew she'd experienced something, but it was hard to say exactly what. A door that wouldn't stay shut and sometimes wouldn't open. A few strange noises, an

33

unexplained smell, and some water on the floor. There might still be a perfectly rational explanation. And what would she do if it really was Grace? No one would believe her. They'd rush her off to the doctor's again and that would be the end of everything.

When she opened the door she was relieved to find the flat quiet. Everything felt perfectly normal. Her magazine was still lying open on the coffee table, just as she'd left it last night. Her jacket was hanging on the back of a chair. What had she expected? To find Grace sitting in the armchair? Maybe Jonathon was right. The old woman should be in a home. She was the one imagining things. Sam had to keep her nerves under control or she'd never be able to stay here.

She picked up her magazine and tried to relax but it was impossible. Too many thoughts spinning around in endless circles. She needed to get out and clear her head. She grabbed her jacket and hurried downstairs.

Sam walked along by the beach huts but there was no one around. Someone had erected a bender in the shelter of a wall and the remains of the fire could still be seen in the derelict garden. A greyhound sniffed at her suspiciously, but soon gave up as she stepped on to the beach. The tide was out and a narrow strip of sand was visible beyond the pebbles. The wind whipped at her hair and caused her jacket to billow.

Sam turned her back on the ruined pier and headed towards Hove. The roar of the waves was strangely comforting and she began to feel calmer. Something caused her to look up and she noticed there was someone sitting on one of the wooden breakers that jutted out into the sea. She looked like a siren that had been left behind by the tide. Sam could just make out the long dreadlocks hanging down her back. She realized it was Jade. She nodded to her as she passed, not sure if Jade would remember who she was or not.

'The primordial waters,' Jade said. 'I bring my crystals

here, whenever they need cleansing.' Sam saw she was holding something floating in the water. 'It's the autumn equinox. A good time to prepare yourself.'

'The equinox? What's that?' Sam asked.

'It's when the light and the darkness are held in balance. Day and night are equal.'

Sam thought about this for a minute. 'Then the darkness will win, won't it?'

'Yes, until the spring. That's Nature's way. We've lost touch with the cycle of the seasons. That's why we're so messed up.'

'I suppose you're right,' Sam said thoughtfully. 'I've never thought about it before.' She looked out at the ocean as if seeing it in a new light.

'Why don't you tell me about it?' Jade said.

'I'm not sure I can.'

'I see things,' Jade announced enigmatically. 'I sense things too, always have. I can see you've been touched.'

'What do you mean?' Sam asked anxiously.

'By the otherworld. It's all around us, only most don't see it.'

'Oh,' Sam said as she hauled herself up on to the jetty. They sat in silence for a few minutes watching the waves. The sun had dropped over the horizon but there was still enough light to make out the two piers in the distance. Jade pulled in a cotton bag that she'd been holding in the water. She let the water drain out, then emptied out a collection of crystals into her palms. She gave one to Sam to hold.

'Amethyst, for protection.'

The wet crystal glittered in her hand. 'I think my flat might be haunted,' she said at last. It didn't sound so crazy, out here in the twilight, with the waves breaking at their feet.

'Probably,' Jade commented, as if Sam had said nothing unusual.

'There's one room. It's . . . ' she hesitated, stuck for

words. 'It's . . . there's something wrong there. I can feel it. The door bangs for no reason. I leave it closed and find it wedged open. There's a smell too. And water. It doesn't sound like much, but I know something doesn't want me there. And I don't know what to do about it.' She knew she sounded pathetic, but she felt relieved she'd told someone.

'Something's troubled,' Jade said matter-of-factly.

'But what can I do?'

Jade shrugged. 'There's different ways. Depends what's there. And what it wants.'

Sam told her about Grace. 'Do you think it's her ghost?' she asked.

'Maybe. It could be lots of things. Sometimes it's the building. Energies get blocked there. It could be anything. I'll need to come and see for myself.'

'You mean you'll help?' Sam said, feeling a surge of hope.

'I will,' Jade said simply.

13

The whole house was in darkness when they arrived. The stairwell stretched above them, leading up to whatever awaited. Twice Jade stopped on the stairs and stood listening. Sam opened the front door nervously, but she couldn't hear anything. It was quiet as the grave, only she wished she hadn't thought that. She switched on the light and led Jade through the living room and down the corridor to the spare room. She was relieved to see the door was still closed.

Jade caught her arm as she went to open it. She moved

Sam aside and stood in front of the door with her eyes closed and her fingertips touching the wood. 'Stay here,' she whispered, after a few minutes. She walked into the room and again stood still for some minutes, as if listening.

Sam could see the pool of water on the floor, though the smell of damp was less overpowering than before. The only light in the room was from the streetlight, filtered through the branches of the tree. It filled the room with shifting shadows that seemed to move with an intelligence of their own. Was that what Jade was seeing? Sam waited impatiently, ready to reach for the light switch if anything happened; though she wasn't sure what she expected.

Jade came out and led her away, back to the kitchen. 'Well,' Sam asked. 'Did you see anything?'

'I didn't see anything specific. But there's a lot of pain in that room, in this house. I could feel it on the stairs too.'

'Then it's everywhere?' Sam said, her heart sinking. 'Is there anything we can do?'

'I can try and seal the room for tonight. I need a couple of candles.'

'Will night lights do?'

'Might be OK.'

'What are you going to do?' Sam asked eagerly.

'There're two dark spots in the room. They're like funnels channelling in negative energies.'

'Where the water appears!'

'And by the door. Think of them like open wounds that need to be cleansed and healed.'

'Can you do it?'

Jade was noncommittal. 'I don't know what we're dealing with yet. If the problem's as old as you say, it won't be easy to heal.'

'Ben told me the flat's been empty for ages. Like there was something here that no one wanted to face.'

'And it may be you too.'

'Me?' Sam was shocked.

'You're the one experiencing it. Maybe you were the trigger.'

Sam was silent. She felt as if she was being sucked into some dark funnel herself and might never manage to get out again. She had a horrible vision of herself spinning endlessly, trapped in some indeterminate world with only Grace for company. All her hopes and plans seemed futile. She'd lived in darkness before, literally so. There'd been whole weeks when she couldn't bear the light. She'd lain in bed in a darkened room, too weak to move, her limbs aching, flinching at the slightest noise. She'd despaired that it would ever end, but it had, hadn't it?

'Look,' Jade told her, 'I'll do what I can, but you have to do your part too. Don't give in to it. Keep your mind focused on the light. Think of something positive, a happy memory, someone you love, anything. Protect yourself.'

14

Despite Jade's advice it wasn't easy to get to sleep that night. She tried to be calm, but she was lying there waiting for something to happen. She strained to hear every slight noise. Was that a footstep? Was that voice really downstairs? She tensed every time a car passed in the street. She left the light on in her room and had to keep opening her eyes to reassure herself she was alone. Eventually, hours later, she dozed off and fell into a troubled sleep. She knew she'd been dreaming, but when she finally got up next morning she couldn't remember any of it. Whatever Jade had done, it had worked. The flat felt different. Even the corridor seemed less gloomy.

Although she hadn't slept well, she found she had more energy today. After breakfast she went along to the local sports centre and signed up to use the gym. She had to take more care of herself, build up her strength, then her nerves wouldn't trouble her so much. She had so many plans, so many things she wanted to do. She had to get on with it, not waste her time thinking about the past. Especially Grace.

Later that afternoon she went down to the seafront to tell Jade the good news. She could hear the drums even before she crossed the main road. Their insistent beat seemed to summon her and she found herself quickening her pace. When she arrived she found Ben among a crowd of people sitting around the fire. A large rusty pan was simmering amid the flames. A mouth watering smell of spices mingled with the smoke, reminding her she hadn't eaten that day.

'The tide'll be just right by Saturday,' Maxine was saying eagerly. She was wearing a striped woolly hat pulled down low over her shaved head. It was the first time Sam had seen her wear any colour other than black.

'Just right for what?' Sam asked.

'The party,' a boy answered. 'On the pier. We climb up there at low tide, party all night, then come down at low tide in the morning.'

'You're joking,' Sam said, looking across to the tall rusty girders that supported the pier decking. 'How would we all get up there?'

'It's not as hard as it looks. We've got a rope ladder,' Ben told her. 'We've already checked it out.'

'The sound system's organized. Chloe's doing the food. People are coming from all over. It'll be wicked. And once we're out there, no one will be able to stop us.' Maxine's eyes were unusually bright. Everyone seemed excited. Sam realized there were more people milling around than she'd ever seen before.

There was no sign of Jade. Sam stayed until sunset, watching the sun go down over the sea before leaving to go home. She was so tired now she was sure she'd sleep. As she approached the steps she heard footsteps hurrying towards her.

'Wait a minute,' Jade shouted.

She arrived out of breath, carrying a small parcel. 'Here,' she said. 'You might need these.'

Sam looked inside the carrier bag and saw an assortment of candles. As far as she could tell in the fading light, some were handmade. 'The flat feels different today,' she said.

'Use them tonight, just in case. Put them in the same place I left the night lights last night. You're sure you don't want me to come with you?'

'No,' Sam insisted. 'I need to get through this on my own.'

'OK, but remember, concentrate on the light.'

Sam felt sure everything was going to be fine. Even as she climbed the stairs the shadow-filled stairwell held no terrors. She walked through the flat confidently, made herself a hot drink and put it next to her bed. Only when she went to open the boxroom door did she feel a slight hesitancy, but she went in bravely, picked up the burnt out night lights and replaced them with Jade's candles. There was no denying the room was still a bit odd. The air might never be fresh; the dampness still lurked in the walls, and maybe more: maybe the walls would always hold the traces of whatever tragedy had happened here. But it wasn't her tragedy. It couldn't touch her.

She lit the candles and watched the flames waver in the draught from the open door. They soon settled, giving off a comforting glow. Then she closed the door behind her and went into her own room. It was a struggle to keep her eyes open. She'd barely touched the cocoa before she fell into a deep sleep.

Across the corridor the boxroom door shuddered in its frame. A cold breath crept through the keyhole, sending an icy chill into her bedroom. Sam shivered in her sleep and pulled the duvet closer. The electric light flickered and grew dim. Shadows gathered round her, watching, wary. Jade's warning must have sunk into her subconscious because in her dream there was bright light. The door to her room was wide open and through it she could see sunshine pouring into the corridor. It was so bright she had to shade her eyes.

She felt something pull at the bedclothes and realized there was a child standing by the side of her bed. She could barely make it out for the glare. The light was getting stronger all the time. It went straight through the child, lingering on her silhouette as if she were on fire. Suddenly the image wavered and vanished, leaving only the sound of laughter getting ever more distant. The light faded too, leaving Sam cold and shivering.

She was no longer in bed. She was still in her pyjamas and her feet were very, very cold. She looked down hoping to find her shoes. With a shock she realized there was water swirling around her feet. Wherever she looked there was nothing but water. There seemed to be no sky, only a bitter wind that whipped at her hair and stung her cheeks. She knew she had to keep walking. Someone was waiting for her and she had to find them. Her feet were cold as ice and it was an effort to keep them moving. The water was rising. It was now slapping around her knees, eerily silent. She was relieved to see a figure emerge from the gloom. How pretty she looked with her bright, flowery dress and her flowing hair. She was standing on the pier, holding out a small, gloved hand towards Sam. Sam couldn't make out her face because it was veiled by her golden hair. She reached out towards her and grabbed at her hand. Icy fingers closed around her wrist, dragging her closer. The glove was wringing wet and green with mould. Sam felt the cold, putrid water drip down her arm and struggled to free herself. Suddenly she saw the figure's face. It wasn't Grace, it was Kate.

41

15

Sam couldn't free herself from that wet, gripping hand. Even when she woke, her fingers felt damp and icy cold. She turned over to look at the clock and was shocked to see it was almost twelve. She sat up in bed and tried to massage some life back into her hand. It was another bright autumn day but there seemed to be no warmth in the sunlight that flooded into the room. Sam felt exhausted, but she knew if she closed her eyes she'd be back in that dream. It was still there, waiting. She didn't know what it meant.

As she began to get up, she put her hand on to the duvet and was shocked to feel a damp patch. She stared at it uncomprehendingly, unwilling to believe her own eyes. There, on the plain cotton cover, was the unmistakable print of a small hand. Sam threw the duvet back and leaped out of bed. She rushed into the corridor and was relieved to see the door to the spare room was still closed. She took a deep breath and pushed it open. The candles had burnt themselves out leaving a dense, waxy smell in the air. The whole room was different. She couldn't explain it, but there was a subtle change, almost as if the colours in the faded wallpaper were growing brighter.

She stepped into the room and went to open the window. The sea must be exceptionally rough because she could hear the waves breaking on the shore. She could even taste the salt on her lips. When she turned round she saw there was something lying on the floor just behind the door. Something that hadn't been there before. She knew what it was even before she bent to pick it up. Knew it would be damp and icy cold to the touch. She stared at it, feeling her blood run cold. Fighting off a feeling of revulsion she took it between her fingers. It was a white cotton glove, too small for her own hand. Three lines of fine stitching decorated the back, but the fingertips were worn threadbare and marked by greenish stains. The whole thing gave off an unpleasantly sweet mouldy smell.

Holding it at arm's length she went into the kitchen and wrapped it in three layers of old carrier bags. A few minutes later she was hurrying towards the seafront, desperately hoping she'd find Jade. She had no one else to turn to. She couldn't tell her family, not even Kate. She knew what they'd think. They'd say that the psychiatrists had been right all along. They'd drag her back to that depressing ward where she'd once been forced to spend a few weeks. Only this time she might never get out again. But the glove was horribly real. You could touch it, smell it. And that cold, gripping hand. She knew now that something had reached out for her. Something had crossed over the boundary between worlds. Past and present, living and dead. Even the cold wind seemed to recall that icy touch. She felt as if there was some invisible barrier between her and the rest of the world; the cars that waited impatiently by the traffic lights, the joggers exercising on the promenade, the pedestrians going about their business. She wanted to cling to each lamp-post, to reach out and touch the people she passed. 'I'm real, I'm here, aren't I?' she wanted to ask.

The seafront was almost deserted apart from a small group of people in the derelict garden. A girl was trying to light a fire but the wind kept putting it out before the flames took hold. They stared at Sam hostilely but one of them pointed out Jade's hut and Sam hurried towards it. As she neared the door she was relieved to hear familiar voices.

'Jade,' she shouted, knocking urgently. She handed her the parcel as soon as the door opened. 'I found this.'

'What is it?' asked Maxine. She was sitting cross-legged on the floor, dressed all in black as usual, apart from the multicoloured bangles on her wrists.

Sam sat down beside her without replying. Jade poured a mug of herbal tea from an old enamel kettle which was steaming on a small camping stove. Sam put her hands around it, grateful for the warmth that slowly spread into her frozen fingers. She shuddered as Jade unwrapped the glove. It seemed to contaminate the whole hut.

'So you had a visitor?' Jade said calmly. 'Did you see her?'

Sam shook her head. 'I found it this morning. She'd been in my room too.' Sam sipped the steaming liquid and grimaced. She'd never liked herbal tea.

'It's weird,' Maxine said looking puzzled.

Sam told her about some of the things that had happened in the room. 'Can you do anything?' she asked Jade anxiously. 'It's getting worse.'

'Maybe that's good,' Maxine suggested. 'Things are coming to a head.'

'I don't know. I don't know what she wants, why she comes.' Sam wasn't sure they weren't all mad.

'If you think about it, the dead outnumber the living. It's surprising we don't notice them more often,' Maxine said solemnly.

'I suppose so. I've never believed in ghosts,' Sam replied. 'Until now.' She smiled wryly at Jade. 'So you think it really was Grace?'

'She died in that room, right?' Maxine butted in eagerly. 'It has to be her. When something really traumatic happens the spirit can't move on.'

'Emotions can bind,' Jade agreed.

'Of course they do,' Maxine continued. 'It's like a web. All the fear, the pain, even the hopes and happy memories, they're all threads in one big web.' She moved her hands expressively as she spoke. Sam watched the Indian bangles slide up and down her wrists. 'It even stretches through time,' she finished.

'And I'm tangled in it,' Sam said wryly.

'So untangle the web, then you'll both be free.'

'You make it sound so easy,' Sam said, suddenly feeling more hopeful. 'What do you think, Jade?'

'If it is Grace, she has to want to move on. Maybe we can help the process of healing, but we can't do it for her. If she doesn't want to let go . . . ' Jade shrugged. She looked at Sam speculatively. 'She wants something from you.'

'I know,' Sam said sadly. 'Only I don't understand what.'

16

They got to the house just as the front door opened. A man in an expensive suit was shaking Jonathon Stacy by the hand.

'I'll let you have the valuation as soon as I can,' he said as he got into his car. 'You won't be disappointed. I can promise you that.'

He looked askance at the trio of Sam, Jade, and Maxine before driving off. Jonathon was more openly hostile.

'What do you want?' he said brusquely.

'We need to see your aunt,' Sam told him.

Jonathon raised his eyebrows. 'Then you'll be disappointed. She's not here. She's in hospital. Had a nasty fall last night. They decided to keep her in for tests.'

'Is she all right?' Sam asked anxiously.

'As well as can be expected. She should be in a home, not wandering around on her own in the middle of the night.'

'What happened?'

'The first signs of dementia. Claims she was with her sister Grace.'

45

Sam inhaled quickly as though she had just received a blow. 'She saw Grace?'

Jonathon frowned. 'You!' he hissed. 'You started this, didn't you? Don't deny it.'

'I don't know what you mean,' Sam said.

'I think you do. You've been stirring up the past. Asking her about Grace. I warned you not to interfere. Telling her ridiculous stories about that room. A load of nonsense. Don't pretend it wasn't you.' He shoved his finger at her face. 'She's just a confused old woman. Should be in a home, but will she go? No. And why? Because of Grace, that's why. Now you come along and make her worse.'

'Maybe she did see Grace,' Sam said quietly.

'Grace is dead. She died before I was born, I told you that.' He spat the words out at her. 'She doesn't come back. The dead don't come back.' He moved towards her threateningly, then seemed to change his mind. 'Well, never mind. Maybe you've done us all a favour. She'll have to go into a home now.' He smiled cynically as he stepped aside to let them pass.

'Who's that?' Maxine asked as they climbed the stairs.

'The old lady's nephew. He can't wait to sell the house.'

'It must be worth a fortune. Poor old thing. I wouldn't want to have him looking after me.' Maxine shuddered.

'He doesn't live here, thank God. He's creepier than any ghost. Imagine bumping into him in the dark!'

They were all laughing as they entered Sam's flat and settled in the big, sunny living room. Maxine took a cushion and sat on the floor while Jade perched on the edge of the armchair as if she'd never used a piece of furniture before.

'We have to warn Ben,' Sam said. 'We can't let Jonathon get away with it. I think she really did see Grace.'

'She was wandering around last night,' Jade said quietly, giving Sam a querying look. 'We don't know where she fell.'

Sam stared at her in dismay. 'You think she was here? That it was her?'

'We have to keep an open mind, that's all I'm saying. She really wants Grace to be here, doesn't she?'

Sam nodded. 'But you've been in the room. You felt it.'

'I felt the pain,' Jade said simply.

'It's Grace's pain,' Sam insisted. 'She died there, remember.'

'It was her room,' Maxine agreed. 'It has to be her.'

Jade shrugged. 'I don't care whose pain it is. This house needs healing. Maybe it's Grace, maybe it's the old woman, maybe it's you,' she finished, looking at Sam.

'It's not me,' Sam retorted. 'I didn't put that glove there.'

'Chill,' Maxine said. 'No one's accusing you of that. You've got to do something, Jade.'

Jade nodded. 'I need time to prepare. We can't just rush in. It's too dangerous.'

'Why not stay with us for a few days?' Maxine said.

'I can't. My sister's coming on Saturday. And anyway, it'd feel like giving up. This is my home now. I've got to stay here.' Sam looked at Jade pleadingly. 'Isn't there anything you can do now?'

'Use the crystals,' Maxine rushed in before Jade had time to answer.

'I'll do what I can, but I can't promise it'll work.'

17

The flat felt suddenly huge and empty when they had gone. Jade had left a few of her crystals placed around the boxroom and had secured the door with some sort of talisman, a small leather pouch stuffed with strong-smelling herbs. It reminded Sam of a particularly nasty medicine she'd once had to take. She tried to shut her thoughts off too. She was too tired to attempt to make sense of it all. She was glad her sister was coming for the weekend. It would help her get a better perspective on things. She rang Kate to finalize the details of her visit. It was good to hear her voice, to talk about normal, trivial things like music and train timetables. When she put the phone down she felt more optimistic. She was sure nothing would happen when Kate was here. She was too full of life.

In the evening Sam went to the gym and worked out for two hours. She made sure she got home before dark. She lit all the lights, played music loudly, baked a potato and forced herself to eat it. To her surprise, she found energy she didn't know she had. Then suddenly, as she washed the last few dishes, she flagged. She hurried down the corridor and into her bedroom, refusing to look behind her. She wasn't the intruder. She was where she belonged: in her own home, in her own time, the present. No one was going to take that away from her. Maybe she was just too tired to worry. It was a relief to slip between the sheets and sink unresistingly into a deep sleep. She didn't notice the spare room door shudder in its frame or the cold air that poured through the keyhole. The handle turned ineffectually until the talisman swung like a pendulum, marking the hours of that other world. Even the crying that went on until dawn couldn't wake her.

On Friday she woke late, still feeling tired, and struggled to get back to the daytime world. Her dreams seemed to have some pull on her, like the moon on the tide. She could only remember disjointed flashes but she was sure Grace had moved through them all, as tied to her as her own shadow. Ignoring the spare room, Sam went through the flat checking each room in turn. Everything was as she'd left it. She felt strangely calm but she knew it wasn't over yet. She sensed the past was waiting to return. Given the chance it would sneak up on her as surely as the tide creeps over the sand.

It was hard to get on with her life. She bought the local paper and tried to look for a job but found it impossible to concentrate. She couldn't do anything. The house wouldn't let her. It dominated her thoughts, absorbed all her energies. She replayed the events of the past week over and over again, but still couldn't find any answers. She wondered if Mrs Armstrong was still in hospital. Was that why she'd had an undisturbed night? Was it her memories that had somehow disturbed the flow of time? Had her delirium spread into the very fabric of the house? Maybe Jonathon was right, though she hated to admit it.

It was late afternoon before she remembered Ben. He probably didn't even know about his gran's accident. Relieved to have found something she could do, she grabbed her jacket and headed for the seafront. She felt the buzz of excitement as soon as she started down the steps. There were more people than ever. The news of the party must have spread. It took her a while to spot Ben. He was down by the water's edge, skimming pebbles over the surface of the water while Hobo splashed around in the shallows, vainly trying to retrieve them. His hair was tied back in a ponytail today, exposing the fragile bone structure of his face. He seemed so happy that she hesitated to spoil his mood, but it had to be done.

They walked back to the promenade and joined the throng of people waiting for food. A girl Sam had never seen before was dishing up food from an ancient van. Ben handed her a plate of vegetable curry and they looked for a sheltered place to sit. The curry was so hot it made her eyes smart. She ate a few mouthfuls before saying, 'You know about your gran?'

He nodded. 'Maxine told me.'

'Jonathon was at the house yesterday,' she said quietly. 'He's had the house valued.'

'He's what? He's got no right to do that.' He threw his plate of food aside, where it was immediately wolfed down by the dogs.

'He insists she'll have to go into a home now. We have to stop him.'

Ben turned away from her and looked out to sea. His face was closed and unreadable.

'There's more, Ben. She thinks she saw Grace, and I believe her.'

He looked at her suspiciously.

'There's something going on in the house. I've heard her. Found things.' When he still didn't say anything she continued, 'You told me you wouldn't live there, remember. We can't just ignore it.'

'Does Jonathon know this?' he said coldly.

'Some of it. Not from me,' she said hurriedly. 'But your gran told him she'd seen Grace and now he thinks she's senile. We have to do something.'

'Keep out of this,' Ben demanded. To Sam's horror he got to his feet and walked away.

18

Sam finished as much of her food as she could. She was shaken by Ben's sudden change of mood. He must know she wouldn't do anything to upset his grandmother. She was trying to help. The sun had dipped below the horizon leaving the sea a pale, misty blue. The shadows were deepening and she realized it would soon be dark. More people had gathered round the fire; many had brought drums and their hypnotic rhythm began to permeate the night.

'You don't have to go back there.' Maxine had come to sit by her. 'Stay with us. Jade'll be back soon.'

Sam shook her head. Maxine touched her wrist. 'We could all go together, later. You don't have to do this alone.'

'I'll be OK,' she said, getting to her feet. 'It's only one night. My sister's coming tomorrow.' Right now the living seemed more of a problem than the dead. Hobo followed her to the steps, circling round her energetically. She bent to pat his tangled head, glad that someone trusted her, before walking up to the main street.

She breathed a sigh of relief when she closed the front door of the house. She needed time to think. It wasn't late, but it was very quiet. No light had been showing from the first floor windows and the ground floor was in darkness, meaning Mrs Armstrong was probably still in hospital. Was she totally alone in the house? She looked up the stairwell trying to see if there was any slither of light escaping from the neighbours' doors, but there was nothing except the ever deepening shadows that waited on each landing.

She pressed the first light switch and began to climb the stairs. With each step the silence became more intense. She jumped when a sudden beam of light swept over her, illuminating the empty stairwell with an awful clarity. Her legs seemed to freeze and she had to force herself to continue. It was only a car. Someone out there in the normal world, going about their business in a safe, normal way that was denied her. Her breathing was short now. The stairs seemed to stretch on forever. She reached the first landing, switched on the next light, dismayed by the darkness that now lay behind her. No one was in. She could feel the emptiness, the absence of any human presence in the large old house.

Her arm shook as she grabbed the banister and continued her ascent, determined not to give in to the fears that threatened to overwhelm her. She couldn't turn back; she didn't belong with the crowd of strangers she'd left on the seafront. They didn't really trust her, not even Jade. Tonight

51

she had to deal with this on her own. Tomorrow Kate would arrive, everything would be different.

As she fumbled for her key in her bag, her fingers found the crystal Jade had given her a few days ago when this had all started. She put it in her jacket pocket and continued her search. While she hesitated the light on the top floor went out. A complete and utter darkness descended. The shock spurred her to action. She ran up the last few remaining stairs and groped at the light switch, finally taking in a great gulp of air when the light came back on. She tried to avoid looking back down the stairwell as she opened her door and hurried inside.

She threw her jacket on to a chair, forgetting about the crystal in the pocket. She didn't notice it fall to the floor and roll across the carpet. For a moment, looking around the large, comfortable room, she felt safe. This was her home now. Then she heard it. A floorboard creaked in the corridor. The old woman's words rang in her ears, 'She does come back . . . You'll hear her.' Sam felt a cold draught on her face. The hairs on the back of her neck stood on end as she heard the boxroom door slowly open.

She moved towards the dark corridor, wishing she'd left all the lights on earlier. Her body resisted each step. Her legs felt stiff and brittle as though they might suddenly break. The temperature was dropping by the minute. The cold became so intense her skin was tingling. She wanted to turn and run. Brave the shadows that waited on the stairs, get out of this flat, this house and never return. But she couldn't do that. She wasn't going to give up now. Suddenly she knew what she had to do. She took a deep breath and called out softly, 'Grace, is that you?'

19

The corridor seemed endless. She felt she'd been walking down it for an eternity. There was no sound from the room, no movement apart from the door swinging slowly back and forth. Sam was shivering violently, but she went on. She hadn't switched on the light. She didn't need to. There was light spilling out of the spare room. A soft, flickering glow unlike the harsh electric light she knew. She hesitated near the threshold of the room, noticing that Jade's talisman had fallen to the floor. Sam waited and listened, but all she could hear was the rhythmic sound of the waves. The sea sounded so close tonight as if it was pounding against the walls, trying to find a way in. She couldn't turn back now. She had to know what was waiting in that room. She had no choice but to push back the door and enter.

She gazed in amazement at the scene before her. Candles burned in two tall wooden candlesticks on the mantelpiece. The remains of a fire still glowed in the narrow iron grate. There were photographs on the walls and the wallpaper was as fresh and bright as the day it was bought. But that wasn't all. There was a girl standing by the window, gazing down at the street. Her clothes and hair were dripping wet. She stood absolutely still as a pool of water spread all around her feet.

'Grace?' Sam whispered.

For a moment it seemed the girl could not hear her. Then, as if in slow motion, she began to turn towards her. She stared straight through Sam as though she didn't exist. Her face had a ghastly pallor, tinged with blue. Tears streamed down her sunken cheeks and there were shadows where her eyes should be.

Sam felt a wave of sympathy for the figure before her. They were both caught in a moment that had somehow escaped the flow of time. There was no way back for the girl. Her world had gone. Sam only hoped her own still existed beyond the confines of the room. The girl began to move towards her. There was a horrible squelching sound as her wet shoes touched the floorboards. The scent of stale seawater wafted across the room. As the candlelight illuminated her face, Sam shrank back against the doorframe. She covered her eyes with her hands, but she had to look. She knew she'd go mad if she didn't.

If this was Grace, her face bore no resemblance to the laughing girl she'd seen in the old photograph. Grief had transformed her. Tears had scarred her cheeks, and her eyes . . . What had happened to her eyes? Sam watched, torn between pity and horror, as the girl slowly drew closer. She seemed so real, so solid. If she reached out she could touch her. Sam could barely believe her eyes. As the girl moved forward the water vanished, leaving no trail of wet footprints in her wake. The bright colours of the wallpaper instantly faded. The candles flickered and grew dim. The photographs on the wall merged back into the shadows. It was as if she was the source of the environment around her.

Grace stopped at the doorway as though confronted by some invisible barrier. She was only inches away from Sam. She sank to her knees and began to wail. It was an awful, eerie noise that made Sam's flesh creep. A wave of terror swept over her. She had to get out of this room or she might be trapped here for ever, in this strange twilight world where time endlessly repeated itself like a loop of film. There was only one problem. Grace barred her way.

20

Grace was still slumped in the doorway, sobbing bitterly. She was rocking back and forth, banging her head on the . . . To Sam's horror she realized it was a door. A door was forming right in front of her eyes. Aware there was no time to delay, Sam stepped forward and pushed past the kneeling figure that was blocking her way. Grace didn't move. She didn't have to. Sam's leg passed straight through her. The last thing she remembered was a searing pain that took her breath away. Then darkness descended over her, dragging her away like a swimmer caught in a current.

She came to some time later, not knowing where she was. Her body ached everywhere and she was so stiff it was difficult to move. Slowly, her eyes adjusted to the dark. She was still in the corridor. She hoped she was dreaming; wished she wasn't hearing that faint persistent sobbing. But no, it was all too real. Suddenly everything came back to her with a terrible clarity. She felt sick. Was she going mad? She couldn't take much more of this. She struggled to her feet and stumbled towards the light switch. She was relieved when light flooded into the corridor and the sobbing stopped.

Sam leaned against the wall for a moment, breathing in the silence. She wondered if she was really alone, or if the other was still waiting, listening, as she was, just beyond the door. Was it over for tonight? She couldn't feel sure. It was still unnaturally cold. Sam shivered every time she remembered that tear-stained face. She didn't think she'd ever feel warm and safe again. She looked at her watch, praying the night was nearly over. It was only three. How many hours until dawn? She couldn't go to bed; she was far too tense. She went into the living room, switched on all the lights and the TV. She curled up on the sofa, staring at the screen without taking anything in.

The noise of the television filled the room. It was comfortingly ordinary. But all the time Sam was listening for those other sounds. She wondered about Grace. What was she doing? Was she still crouched by the door, wet and shivering? And what if the door couldn't hold her? She could sense that other world was still there, waiting its opportunity to return. And if it did? What would happen to her then?

21

'Wake up, Kate, come on.' The phone had been ringing for ages. Why didn't she pick it up? Sam had to talk to someone and Kate was the only one she could trust. She knew she would believe her. At last, someone was answering sleepily.

'Is that you, Sam? What's the matter? Are you all right?'

It was a relief to hear her voice. 'Yes, well, no. I don't know. Something's happened, I've been awake all night.'

'Sam.' Kate sounded desperately worried. 'What's wrong?'

'It's not easy to talk about, but . . . but . . . ' Sam paused, unable to articulate the words she needed to say. She could barely believe it herself and she had seen it. She shuddered at the memory.

'Go on, Sam, please. You have to tell me.' Kate was wide awake now and full of concern.

'It's this flat. It's . . . it's haunted.' She rushed the words out. Now she'd said it she felt calmer.

'Wow, you mean you've really seen a ghost? That's wicked. Do you think I'll see it too?'

'It's not much fun, believe me. It was awful. The worst night of my life. I don't think I can stay here. I can't face another night like that. It was a nightmare.'

'Sam, I'm sorry. Calm down. It's almost morning now, isn't it? Nothing will happen now. You're safe. I'll be—'

'No, I don't feel safe. I've found things, heard things, even in daylight. She's here, I know she is.' The words were tumbling out. There was so much to tell Kate she didn't know where to begin.

Kate didn't reply straight away. She'd never known Sam to be in such a state. Even in the worst months of her illness she'd never been like this. 'Look, I'll get an early train. We'll think of something. Just get out of there, promise. I'll ring you from the train and you can meet me at the station.'

'OK, you're right. I can't stay here. I'm so glad you're coming this weekend. It'll be great to see you.'

Sam knew there was an all night café in town. As she walked through the deserted streets she felt immunized against fear. Nothing in this world would ever worry her again. The café was empty apart from a young couple too engrossed in each other to notice her. She ordered toast and coffee, found herself a table, and sat turning the pages of a magazine.

It was almost nine when she arrived at the station. It was reassuringly busy. Commuters paced impatiently up and down the forecourt, checking their watches every few seconds. Sam waited at the barrier; she wanted to see Kate the second she got off the train. It seemed to take an age for the train to pull in alongside the long, curved platform. Sam was only half aware of the people crowding round her, pushing to get through the narrow gate in the barrier. She was carried through with them on to the platform. She was relieved to see Kate getting out of a carriage near the front.

'Kate, am I pleased to see you,' she told her as they hugged.

'Come on, let's get out of here and you can tell me all about it. You look awful.'

'Thanks. I knew you'd cheer me up,' Sam replied, laughing. 'Let's go down to the beach. So much has happened; I feel like I've been here for months, not just a couple of weeks.'

'I've missed you,' Kate said. 'It's been awful at home without you. Mum fusses all the time.'

'Wait until I tell you everything. You might wish you were back there.'

'I doubt that. At least your life isn't boring.'

'No, it certainly isn't that.'

They arrived at the seafront, crossed the main road, and went down the stairs to the lower promenade. They found a sheltered spot and sat looking out at the sea. The tide was on its way out. Gulls prowled the beach, scavenging among the debris left behind by the waves. The air was so fresh and clean that Sam began to feel more awake.

'You know,' she said to Kate, 'I can't believe it all really happened.'

Kate looked at her anxiously and waited for her to continue. She was looking terrible. There were dark shadows under her eyes and her hair seemed lank and unwashed. For the first time she felt a flicker of doubt. What would she do if Sam was getting ill again? She couldn't leave her here alone, but she couldn't betray her either.

There was a long pause while Sam gazed at the ruined West Pier. In the end she sighed and said quietly, 'That's where I saw her first.'

Kate followed her eyes. She shivered as she looked at the derelict buildings and broken railings. It was all too easy to imagine ghosts sheltering there. She listened in silence while Sam told her all about Grace.

'Then I found this,' Sam said, handing her sister a small package.

'What is it?' Kate asked as she unwrapped the plastic that

covered it. She held it at arm's length, her nose twitching at the mouldy smell.

'It belonged to her,' Sam said, avoiding looking at the small glove until Kate had wrapped it up again.

'This is what you found in the flat? Are you sure it wasn't there all the time? Maybe you just hadn't noticed it.'

Sam frowned. 'Of course not,' she retorted crossly. 'The room was empty. Don't look at me like that, Kate. You have to believe me. I saw her. I've heard her before, sensed her. I've felt the cold, the hostility; but last night I saw her as clearly as I see you now.'

'I do believe you,' Kate answered, not absolutely truthfully. 'Do you think she was murdered? Maybe she's seeking revenge. She can't rest,' she added in a spooky voice.

'It's not funny, Kate. You wouldn't laugh if you'd seen her. I don't know how she died. I think she starved herself when her fiancé died in the war. But why was she all wet and dripping? That was what made it all so awful.' She shuddered at the memory before continuing, 'I have to find out what really happened to her.'

'Try and put it out of your mind, Sam. You have to take care of yourself. We'll talk more later, when you're less stressed.' She put her arm around her and gently rubbed her back. 'I'm cold. And hungry too. Have you got anything to eat?' Kate was already getting to her feet. 'I can't wait to see the flat.'

'All right. I have to face it some time. Let's get it over with.'

22

When they arrived at the house Sam saw a window was open on the ground floor. She hoped that meant Mrs Armstrong was back from the hospital. She really didn't want to bump into Jonathon now.

'It's huge,' Kate said admiringly as she walked into the living room. 'You are lucky. Oops, sorry. I didn't mean . . . '

'I know,' Sam smiled at her. 'I thought so too until things started happening. Wait until you've spent a night here, then see if you still think I'm lucky.' Somehow with Kate here things didn't seem so bleak. It was a lovely flat; if only she wasn't sharing it with a ghost.

'So show me the room,' Kate said eagerly, heading for the corridor. 'I'm dying to see it.' Suddenly she started to shout, 'Grace, where are you? I'm coming.'

'Kate, shut up. Stop it,' Sam scolded.

'What was that?' Kate asked, suddenly looking worried too.

'I didn't hear anything. Go on, you wanted to see the room.'

Kate paused with her hand on the door knob, then knelt down and stared through the keyhole. 'I think I saw something move,' she whispered.

'Stop messing around.' A shiver passed up Sam's spine. 'Are you going in or not? I can't stand here all day.' She couldn't bear to stay near the room, even in daylight it gave her the creeps.

Kate opened the door a fraction and looked in. Suddenly the door swung open and banged against the bedroom wall. Kate jumped and turned white as a sheet.

'I'm not frightened,' she said doubtfully. 'It smells a bit, doesn't it?'

'Let's go, Kate.'

'All right. I am starving. And things don't happen in daylight, do they? Only after dark.' Kate had recovered her confidence now. Sam wasn't so sure. Was it her imagination, or was the room growing colder?

Kate chatted brightly all the way through breakfast, determined to cheer her sister up. Soon Sam knew everything that had happened at home in the past fortnight. They sat in the kitchen drinking mugs of coffee and making plans for the weekend.

'There's a party on the pier tonight,' Sam told her.

'We are going, aren't we? Come on, Sam. It'll do you good to have some fun.'

'Maybe. We'll have to climb on to the pier at low tide. We'll be stuck there all night.'

'Fantastic. We have to go. Anyhow, at least you'll get away from the ghost there.'

'OK.' Sam gave in, smiling. She didn't feel so tired any more. 'I think I'll have a bath. Will you be OK? Promise you won't do anything stupid.'

'Me, really. Don't you trust me?'

'No. I know you too well.'

She left Kate watching TV and went to run a bath. She was glad she wasn't alone. It was such a relief to have Kate here. She stepped into the warm, fragrant water and slowly began to relax. Her eyes started to feel heavy. She'd just shut them for a moment. She must have dozed off because when she opened them again the water was lukewarm. She got out of the bath and wrapped herself in a large towel.

'Kate,' she called. 'Everything OK?'

'Yes, I'm fine,' Kate shouted back.

Sam dried herself and dressed quickly, then walked up the corridor to the living room. Kate was curled up on the sofa. Sam was pleased to see she'd taken her boots off. She must have decided to get changed as her jeans and fleece were thrown over the arm of one of the chairs.

'Like your new dress,' she said, turning over on the sofa.

'What?' Sam mumbled.

'Your new dress,' Kate repeated, smiling mischievously.

'What are you talking about? I haven't—' Sam stopped dead in her tracks as she caught sight of Kate. She had on a long summer dress patterned with bright pink roses and big yellow daisies. Sam shuddered.

'Not your usual style, is it?' Kate said. 'A bit old-fashioned. What's the matter? Sam?'

'Get it off,' Sam whispered. Her words were barely audible. 'Get it off now.' She rushed over to Kate and pulled at her arm.

'All right. Don't make a scene. What is it, Sam?' Kate had suddenly noticed how strange her sister looked. White as a— 'You haven't seen her again, have you?' she asked as she pulled the dress over her head.

Sam grabbed the dress and held it at arm's length. Her hands were shaking.

'Where did you find it?'

'You left it on the chair,' Kate replied, looking puzzled.

'Which chair?'

'Look, what's going on? Why all these questions?' Kate said crossly. 'It's only a dress.'

'No it isn't. It's hers.'

'You don't mean . . . ' Kate's voice faltered.

Sam nodded. She felt more in control now. 'It was her favourite dress. Grace made them herself. Mrs Armstrong told me about them. That's how I met her, she was in that room, her arms full of dresses. It's getting worse, I know it is.'

'I'm all right. Really, I am,' Kate assured her. She'd finished dressing now and was back in her jeans.

'You don't understand,' Sam said. 'It wasn't there. It wasn't there when we came in. It must have appeared when we were in the kitchen or . . . ' Sam stopped. She'd meant to say when you called her, but didn't want to worry Kate more than necessary.

'What about this Mrs Armstrong? You said she had the dresses. Doesn't she have the key?' Kate said calmly. She was trying hard to be sensible. 'She could have come in while we were in the kitchen. We had the radio on, remember. Put the dress down, Sam.'

Sam looked surprised. She gazed at the dress as if she'd forgotten she was still holding it. She threw it on to a chair quickly. 'Yes,' she said doubtfully, 'maybe she is back from hospital. I wish you hadn't put it on, Kate. You have to be more careful. Don't take risks. We don't know what we're dealing with.' She wasn't going to let anything happen to Kate.

'You think she's really dangerous?'

'I don't know,' Sam replied firmly, 'but I'm going to find out.'

23

'What are you going to do?' Kate asked anxiously as Sam started towards the door.

'You'll see. Hurry up.'

Kate looked at her sister with concern. She'd never seen her look like this before. She reached for Sam's arm and said gently, 'You need to rest. You don't want to . . . ' She stopped awkwardly, unable to finish the sentence.

Sam turned round to face her. 'I know,' she said. 'I need to rest, but I can't. Not yet. I'm not ill. You have to believe me.'

'I do believe you, Sam. And I'm here to help. I won't let you down, but you have to take care of yourself. Whatever it is can wait. You must sleep. Please,' Kate pleaded.

Sam hesitated. 'I have to do this,' she said finally. 'I can't sleep. Not until I find out the truth about Grace.' She pulled her arm free and started down the stairs.

'Oh, all right,' Kate sighed as she followed her.

Sam knocked loudly on Mrs Armstrong's door. 'I hope Jonathon's not here,' she said. 'He usually visits on Saturdays.'

The door opened a fraction and the old lady peered at them through the gap. She was holding on to a walking frame and one of her hands was badly bruised. 'Oh, it's you, dear. Come in.'

'I have to talk to you,' Sam told her as they followed her into the stuffy living room. She was walking more slowly than ever, barely able to lift her feet. 'This is my sister Kate.'

'Have a seat. Can I get you a drink? A biscuit?' Mrs Armstrong's arms shook as she lowered herself into her favourite chair.

'I've seen her,' Sam said. 'I've seen Grace. You have to tell me everything. I need to know. What really happened?'

The old lady nodded her head. Her eyes filled with tears. 'Yes, I suppose you do. I try to remember her as she was. Just a minute, I've a photo here somewhere.' She fished around in the large handbag that always hung from the arm of her chair and brought out the photo she'd shown Sam before. Sam glanced at it and passed it to Kate.

'It's the dress,' Kate whispered, turning a shade paler.

'And this was Robert, Bob we all called him. Grace met him at a dance on the pier. Even mother liked him.' She handed Sam a second photo where he was standing next to his plane.

'I thought your mother didn't approve?' Sam asked.

'Not of the engagement, no. But she liked him all right. He was going to be a doctor, you see. He was a good catch. That's what we called it in those days. Of course, Grace could have had anyone she wanted. She had all the boys running after her.'

64

Sam looked at the young airman in the photo. He had his cap under his arm and his hair was shiny with Brylcream. He didn't look much older than Grace; far too young to fight a war.

'What happened when he died?' Sam asked gently.

Mrs Armstrong put the photos back in her bag and snapped it shut. Her hands were trembling. 'One day there was a knock at the door. It was his father. He just handed over the telegram to mother and they went into the living room, this room, and shut the door behind them. Grace had heard him arrive. She rushed downstairs and into the room. I heard the screams. When I went in everything was in chaos. Mother said, "Take her upstairs. She's hysterical." So I took her up to her room.' The old lady stopped speaking, put her hands over her face and began to sob.

'I'm sorry,' Sam said, 'but I have to know. What happened next?'

'She never got over it. At first we all thought she just needed time. But she didn't get any better. She stopped eating. Locked herself in her room. She looked terrible. Her hair began to drop out . . . her lovely golden hair.'

Sam listened carefully. She sensed the old lady was holding something back. She waited a moment for Mrs Armstrong to recover then asked, 'If she locked herself in, why is her ghost so desperate to get out? And why was she so wet?'

24

Mrs Armstrong looked startled. 'You've really seen her?' she asked, brushing the tears from her face.

'Yes, she came last night.'

'I've never seen her. She never forgave me, you see.'

'Forgive you? What for?' Sam was puzzled.

'It wasn't my fault. I did all I could. I tried to help her. But mother insisted. She said the door had to stay locked. It was the war. People were dying all the time. You just coped. You didn't go to pieces.'

'She was locked in the room?' Kate asked horrified.

'In the end, yes.'

'But why?' Sam and Kate asked in unison.

'Because no one in our family had ever gone mad. Mother refused to send her to the psychiatric hospital. Said there was nothing wrong with her that common sense couldn't cure. The noise was heartbreaking. Sometimes she cried all night. I heard it all. My room was just next door. I heard everything. I felt so helpless.' Mrs Armstrong had started to cry again.

'I still don't understand,' Sam said. 'How did she die?' She looked across at Kate who was sitting on the edge of her chair.

'Everything was so different then,' Mrs Armstrong sobbed. 'There wasn't anything I could do. We took food up every day, but she wouldn't touch it. She said she had nothing to live for. Mother said that was wicked. A sin. She said Grace would start eating again when she was hungry enough. But she never did.'

'She was anorexic,' Kate said sympathetically.

'That's what they call it these days, I know. But no one

had heard of it then. It was the war, you see. People were dying every day. A bomb went off just up the street. Killed twelve people just like that. Mother was ashamed of her. Said she ought to be thankful she was still alive. She said women always had to suffer and there was nothing new about that.' Mrs Armstrong had stopped crying now. She put her crumpled hanky down on the side table next to her chair and sat in silence, brooding on her memories.

Sam and Kate looked at each other. They were both sickened by the story they had heard. It was hard to believe people could be so cruel.

'Poor Grace,' Sam said quietly. 'No wonder she's still trapped now.'

'What can we do?' Kate asked. 'How can we free her?'

'I've tried to make her happy,' Mrs Armstrong said, calmer now. 'I've kept all her things. All the things she loved. Her pretty dresses. She made them herself, you know.'

'But her room's empty. Where are all her photos; the ones she had on the wall?' Sam asked.

'That was her punishment, you see.'

'Her punishment?' Sam wasn't sure she'd heard right.

'For not coming out of her room. Mother said she couldn't live in the past. Bob was dead and it was about time she got used to it. I tried my best. I managed to save a few photos. You will tell her, won't you? I've done everything I could. Now Jonathon says he's going to sell the house and I don't know what I can do.'

'Does Jonathon know all this?' Sam asked.

'He's not interested. He only cares about the money. He wants to put me in a home. I won't go. They can't make me, can they?' Mrs Armstrong became very agitated and started to pull her hanky into shreds.

'No, of course they can't,' Sam reassured her.

'I hope she'll be OK,' Sam said as they climbed the stairs to her flat.

'At least we know the truth now.'

'Do we? I'm not so sure. I had the feeling she was holding something back. We still don't know why she was so wet.'

'I forgot about that,' Kate said.

'You wouldn't if you'd seen her. I don't think I'll ever forget. I'll be living with that image for ever.'

'Sorry,' Kate said guiltily.

They remained silent as they went up the last flight of stairs. 'Why didn't you ask her about the water?'

'I did, remember. But after all that stuff about her family she was so upset I couldn't risk making her worse.'

'What are we going to do about Grace?' Kate sounded deflated.

'We'll think of something. We have to. Imagine, suffering like that for all those years. No wonder she looked so awful.'

'I still don't see what we can do. Don't we need a priest or something?'

'Jade will help.'

'What?'

'Jade. She's one of Ben's friends. You'll meet her tonight at the party.'

25

Sam hadn't thought about Ben all day. Now, as she put her eye make-up on, she wondered what sort of mood he'd be in tonight. Would he still blame her for his gran's accident? Anyhow, Ben was the least of her problems. She wasn't going to waste any energy worrying about him.

She looked at the pile of discarded clothing on her bed.

All her clothes seemed so boring. She'd been out so little during her own illness that she'd never needed any party clothes. In the end she pulled on a favourite pair of jeans and a sparkly top that Kate had bought her last Christmas. She rubbed some gel into her hair and pinned it up in a tight knot, then added an extra layer of eyeliner to her eyes. Despite everything, she was starting to look forward to the party.

'Kate, are you nearly ready?' she shouted as she walked up the long corridor. She kept her eyes turned away from the boxroom door.

'Almost,' Kate answered, holding out her hands. The nails had been painted silver. 'Like my new outfit?'

'It's startling. You'll certainly get noticed in that. Remember we have to climb on to the pier.'

'No problem. I've got my boots on. I can't wait to get there. It's so exciting.'

Sam burst out laughing. 'You know, you're right. It is really exciting. I'm making up for lost time.'

'Did you really hate it?' Kate asked quietly. 'You never talked much about being ill.'

'I thought it would never end,' Sam paused, 'but it has. I'm fine now.'

'Of course you are.' Kate picked up her jacket and linked her arm through her sister's. 'Nothing's going to stop us having a good time tonight.'

It was getting dark as they neared the pier. They could hear the sound of drums mingled with the incessant rhythm of the waves. A small crowd of people stood on the promenade, watching the action. Sam and Kate crossed the pebbled beach and joined the queue waiting to climb up on to the pier. A homemade rope ladder hung down from the walkway, anchored by two people at each end.

'Sam,' a voice shouted. She looked up and saw Ben

approaching. She was relieved he'd forgotten his strange mood of the evening before.

'Ben, meet Kate.'

'I came to escort you both to the party.' He held out his arms to them and bowed exaggeratedly. He was wearing an ancient tailcoat and leather trousers. He pushed his way through the crowd until they reached the ladder. 'Who wants to go first?' he said.

'I do,' Kate shouted. 'What's it like up there? Is it dangerous?' Her eyes glowed with excitement.

'Very,' Ben replied. 'It's all right once you get to the concert hall,' he pointed to the building halfway down the pier, 'but you need to watch where you put your feet on the deck. The wood's really rotten.'

'Wait for me when you get to the top,' Sam shouted. Kate was already two thirds of the way up the ladder. It swayed perilously in the wind, but that didn't bother her.

'See you later,' she yelled as she vanished over the top.

'After you,' Ben said, holding the ladder steady. Sam felt a thrill of excitement as she climbed the first few rungs. A year ago she couldn't even climb the stairs to her bedroom without feeling really exhausted. As she neared the top Hobo stuck his head through the railings. Someone gave her a pull up the last few rungs and she found herself on the deck. There was no sign of Kate.

The tide was coming in fast. The waves were now breaking a few feet from the ladder. Ben joined her a couple of minutes later and they made their way towards the old concert hall. It looked pale and ghostly with candlelight flickering dimly through the broken windows. Dark shadows danced furiously within.

'This is where it gets dangerous,' Ben said. Sam could see the water glimmering darkly through the gaps in the decking. They skirted a section where the wood was so rotten the floorboards had totally collapsed. The sound of the drums was getting louder all the time.

'What's that smell?' Sam asked.

'The gulls. There's thousands of them here. Luckily it's not nesting season so they shouldn't attack. You don't notice it after a while.'

'I need to talk to you,' Sam said.

'We are talking,' Ben replied. He looked uncomfortable. 'We'll talk later, I promise.'

'No,' Sam insisted. 'We have to talk now. Something's happened. I saw her.'

Ben's face froze. He turned away from her and looked out towards the horizon. Sam's heart sank. Was he shutting her out again?

'Ben,' she whispered. 'I can't ignore this. I have to do something.'

'I don't know much,' he said after what seemed like minutes. 'We can go further out. It'll be quieter.'

They skirted the concert hall and arrived at a second walkway which led to the final section of the pier. There was another building here, an old pavilion, just as sad and decrepit as the first.

'She met him here, didn't she?' Sam asked.

'Did she? I've no idea. We don't talk about her, believe it or not. Careful, don't go too near the edge. There's no railing here.'

Ben took her arm and steered her towards an entrance at the side of the building. He struck a match and they heard the sound of wings as a hundred seagulls swept round the empty building and out into the night. 'Up here. There's a terrace at the top. No one will disturb us up there.'

Sam pinched her nose as they went up a narrow, winding staircase where the smell was overpowering. The match had burnt out and it was pitch dark. Ben had hold of her hand and she followed blindly. They didn't speak until they were out under the night sky.

'Has your grandmother always lived there?' Sam asked.

'Most of her life. She moved out when she got married,

but then her mother died and she inherited the house. My grandfather wanted to sell it, but she wouldn't have it. They argued about it for years and in the end she had to compromise. The upstairs was divided into flats and rented out.'

'All except my flat.'

They sat in silence for a while. They were sheltered from the wind but above them heavy clouds raced across the newly dark sky. Neither of them really wanted to talk about the past. Sam was the first to speak. 'I want to stay here,' she said. 'I can't go back home. You don't know how hard it was for me to get away.' She felt Ben's eyes watching her.

'I'm listening,' he said.

'I was very ill, for years. I had ME, but no one knew that at first. They couldn't find anything wrong. I had so many tests it was a nightmare. In the end they sent me to a psychiatrist. That was the worst. He almost convinced me I was mad. Everything was too much. I couldn't stand the slightest noise. Sunlight drove me crazy. I was living in the shadows. And I was so tired. Exhausted, all the time.'

'So what happened? You're OK now aren't you?' Ben asked gently.

'I think so.' She paused. 'No, I'm sure. I am all right. I'm so much stronger now. In the end we found a specialist. My mother saw him on TV and wrote to him. I was in hospital for months, but I started to get better. Slowly. So, you see, I can't go back. That would be to give up everything I've worked so hard for.'

'You won't have to,' Ben assured her. They'd moved closer together and without being sure how it happened, Sam found herself kissing him.

They sat looking out over the dark ocean, watching the moonlight reflected in the water. Neither of them noticed the cold.

'She's drawn to you,' Ben said after a few minutes. 'You know that, don't you?'

'So people keep telling me.'

'No one else has seen her. Maybe she thinks you'll understand.'

'I want to help her. No one's ever done that. That's why she died in the first place.'

'Tell me what you saw,' Ben asked quietly. 'What did she look like? I've never even seen a photo of her. Hope told me they were all destroyed after her death.'

'No, not all. Your grandmother has a few.'

'I suppose I was never that interested in her. It's only in the last few years that Gran's started to talk about her. That's when Jonathon started to say she was going senile. Every time she mentions Grace she puts herself one step nearer to the old people's home.'

'In the photo she just looks very young and happy. It's not a close-up so you can't see her that clearly. But, last night . . .' Sam shuddered at the memory. 'She was different. Horrible. And the room was different too.'

'Different? How?'

'I think I saw the room as it was. There were photos on the walls. Candles burning. A fire in the grate. But her eyes, her face. I never want to see that again.' Sam closed her eyes and laid her head on Ben's shoulder. They remained silent for a few minutes, then Sam said, 'What I don't understand is why she was so wet.'

'But I thought you knew,' Ben said in surprise. 'She killed herself by jumping off this pier.'

26

Sam pulled away from him and stared at his face, trying to make out his expression in the feeble light.

'Sam, what's wrong?' he asked anxiously.

'But she died in that room. She was locked in. She stopped eating. That's why she still comes. She can't escape.'

'Maybe I'm wrong.' Ben tried to calm her. 'Look, don't get so upset. I told you I don't know much about her.'

'No, you're right. You must be.' Sam hesitated. She didn't want to offend him, but she had to ask, 'Why would your grandmother lie to me?'

'She's old. Perhaps she just got confused. Look, let's forget about Grace. Enjoy the party. We can't do anything now anyhow.'

Sam made an effort to smile at him. 'You're right, I'd better see what Kate's up to as well.'

'Come on. The party should be in full swing. Look how high the tide is. They'll never get us off here now.'

They left the terrace and made their way carefully back through the pavilion and out on to the deck. They weren't alone any more. Small groups of people sat drinking in the shelter of the walls, watching the waves break over the railing. She realized the water was much higher than before. The narrow walkway that led back to the concert hall was almost totally engulfed by the waves. As they walked she could see the dark water swirling hungrily beneath the decayed floorboards, as though just waiting its chance to engulf them all.

They waited until the waves had peaked then raced, laughing, down the length of the walkway towards the concert hall. Spray showered over them. There was a great roar as a wave behind them reared up ready to break. 'Quick,' Ben shouted, grabbing her hand and pulling her forward as the water swept over the deck and swirled around their feet. Sam felt it pulling her towards the edge. Involuntarily, she thought of Grace. She must have been desperate to welcome its cold embrace. She shivered and forced herself to run as she'd never run before.

They reached the relative safety of the building, wet and elated. Sam wasn't afraid any more. So much had happened in the past twenty-four hours her life would never be the same again. She felt ready for anything, even the ghost of Grace. Someone had set up a barbeque in a corner of the concert hall and the smell of smoke and sausages wafted across to them.

'I'm hungry,' Ben said. 'I'll be back in a minute.'

'OK,' Sam told him. 'I'll find Kate. She's probably in here dancing.'

Sam peered into the crowd of dancers but she didn't recognize anyone. She pushed her way through. The noise was deafening. About twenty people with drums had gathered together and their music seemed infused with the frenzy of the wind and the sea. It was hard to believe that not far away the town still existed, with its paved streets and traffic and electric lights. Sam felt they'd all been transported to some more elemental world where anything might happen.

Where was Kate? Suddenly someone grabbed her arm. Relief rushed over her and she turned around smiling only to be disappointed. It wasn't Kate, it was Jade.

'She's here,' she shouted. 'Hurry.'

They fought their way through the crowd towards the nearest exit. The narrow walkway that led to the pavilion was impassable now. If Kate was out there Sam hoped she'd have the sense to wait until the tide receded before venturing back.

'Look,' Jade said, 'there she is.'

Sam peered into the darkness. A shadowy silhouette seemed to be moving through the breaking waves. It was hard to see anything clearly. 'No,' she protested. 'Kate? No, get back . . . '

'She's waiting for you,' Jade whispered.

Another huge wave broke over the walkway. Sam felt the decking shudder under its onslaught. Spray flew everywhere. She could just make out the shape of a figure, her long skirts billowing around her in the wind.

'That's not Kate,' Sam said.

'Who's Kate?' Jade whispered.

'My little sister. She's here somewhere.'

They watched the figure walk towards them, unaffected by the waves that cascaded over her shimmering form. Sam could just make out the roses on her dress which clung to her like a gaily patterned shroud. The long golden hair was a mass of damp, dripping tangles. She sensed the determination that impelled her ever forwards, in defiance of the elements and all the laws of time and space. Sam clung to the broken railing, relieved to feel the rust rub against her palm and the cold, wet metal remain firm beneath her fingers.

The figure seemed tied to the rhythm of the waves. The image ebbed and flowed as if it could not hold fast to the reality it sought. At times the outline gave way, leaving only the seething ocean where a cheek or an arm should be. Sam felt sick and dizzy. She knew she too was in danger of being dragged away to some terrible world where nothing was solid and safe and everything was sucked into a never ending cycle of pain and sorrow.

'Sam,' Jade whispered, trying to loosen her grip on the rail. 'Let's go.'

Sam ignored her. She couldn't let go of the only thing that anchored her to the world she knew. Just as she couldn't close her eyes or turn her face away from the thing that so horrified her even as it drew closer and closer.

'Remember Kate,' Jade ordered. 'We have to find her. Come on.'

Panic stricken, Sam turned to face her friend. She felt the life flood back into her limbs. 'What if she's out there?' she whispered.

'I don't think so.' Jade closed her eyes and concentrated. 'I don't think she's here at all.'

'Where is she? No, she promised . . . '

'She's there. In the flat. I'm sure of it.'

27

Kate had left the party an hour earlier. She'd watched Sam and Ben go off on their own and guessed they would not miss her for a while. She was pleased to see her sister so happy. She deserved some good luck after all she'd been through. She'd joined in the throng of dancers trying to let the beat of the music carry her away, but something stopped her. An idea had formed in the back of her mind and the more she thought about it the more convinced she became that it was the right thing to do. Sam really needed her help. It would be a disaster if she had to go back home now. No one would believe her. People didn't believe in ghosts any more. It was so unfair that this should happen to Sam of all people. She said she was OK, but Kate could see that wasn't really true. She was just trying to be brave. Her sister wasn't strong enough to fight anybody, let alone a ghost. She'd look out for Sam, take care of her.

Kate looked around, wishing there was someone she

could ask to go with her; but she didn't know anyone. She went back to where the rope ladder had been left on the decking and started to throw it over the side. The bottom now dangled in the water, but it was only a couple of feet to the shore. She'd just have to get her feet wet. Lucky, really, that her skirt was so short.

Kate had just started to climb over the railing when a voice shouted, 'Stop.' She looked back and saw a boy running towards her.

'Wait,' he said. 'The ground slopes really steeply here. That water's much deeper than it looks.'

'Thanks,' Kate told him, looking down on the breaking waves. 'But I have to do it.'

'The party's that bad, eh?' he said smiling. 'Don't worry. I'll help. You have to swing the ladder over the beach then jump off.'

She waved goodbye as she started to climb down. She could feel the spray soaking her tights and the waves did look much higher from this perspective.

'Go on. Now,' the boy shouted.

Kate let the ladder sway in the wind for a minute, then pushed towards the shore as hard as she could. As she neared the beach she tried to loosen her grip on the ropes but it wasn't easy. Too late. She hadn't been quick enough and the ladder was now swinging back out to sea. An icy wave broke over her feet and water crept up the back of her legs. She clung determinedly, feeling the rope fibres grate against the tender skin on her palms. Her fingers were going numb with the cold. She could hear the stones being dragged unresistingly by the current and couldn't stop herself imagining what it would be like if she fell.

'Hurry up,' the boy yelled down at her.

Kate looked behind her and shuddered. There was a huge wave rearing up a few metres away. The thought of Sam mobilized her. She swung out as fast as she could, freeing one foot as she went. It was now or never. She held her breath and leapt, impelling herself through the air with a desperate determination to clear the waves.

She was relieved to feel the cold, damp pebbles bruise her knees as she landed. She scrambled to her feet just as the wave crashed to shore behind her. Her feet slid back into the surf and she felt the ground being sucked away from under her. She threw herself forward and stumbled up the steep slope to the promenade. She felt in her pocket to make sure the key was still there, then started to climb the stairs to the main road. She looked back at the pier with a pang of regret, but there was no turning back now. Sam needed her help and she wouldn't let her down.

28

'I have to get home, quick.' Sam was in distress. She'd searched everywhere for Kate although in her heart she knew she wouldn't find her. She always did rush into things. What did she know about dealing with ghosts? She might make everything worse. 'How could she? She promised me she wouldn't do anything stupid. How can I get off here? I'll have to swim.'

'I'll come with you,' Jade reassured her. 'There is a way off, but it's dangerous.'

'We have to hurry,' Sam urged.

'Come on, this way,' Jade said grimly. 'We can get on to the metal walkway that leads to the promenade. We just have to find a way round the security gates.'

They hurried towards the edge of the decking, climbed over a pile of loose timber, and found themselves in an area where the railing and most of the floorboards had fallen away. Sam was confronted by a vertiginous drop down to the waiting sea. Water surged restlessly around the metal supports and spray filled the air. A few metres away a huge gate barred the way to the promenade. When Sam saw the coils of barbed wire wreathed around it her heart sank.

'It's OK,' Jade told her, reading her mind. 'We can get underneath it. I've done it once before, when we squatted the pier last summer. Once we get to the walkway it's easy.' She knelt down and examined the exposed structure carefully. 'We can make a bridge here,' she said at last. 'Get some of those planks.'

Sam sorted through the pile of loose timber, pulling out the longest lengths and testing their strength as best she could. Some snapped as soon as she put any pressure on them, but a few were strong enough for their purpose. She dragged them back to Jade and together they began to guide them across the gaps in the decking until a narrow bridge was formed. Just looking at it made Sam feel dizzy.

'Let's go,' she said impatiently.

'We could make it wider.'

'No, we haven't time. And anyway, it would still be terrifying. Let's get it over with.'

Thinking of Kate and what she'd say to her when, if ever, they finally found her, Sam put a foot on the improvised bridge. The timber wobbled as soon as she put any weight on it but she took a few deep breaths and edged forward, inch by inch. Then, halfway across, the timber creaked menacingly and she was sure it was about to break. She lost concentration and swayed momentarily, suddenly aware of the waves pounding far below.

'Don't look down,' Jade shouted. 'You're almost across.'

Sam made a huge effort and managed to steady herself. A few more steps and she would be able to reach the rail at the other side. It took all her willpower not to give in to the pull of gravity and just let herself drop down to the waiting sea.

Those few steps seemed to take an eternity and she knew if she made it she'd never be afraid of anything again. At last, the railing was within her reach. She grabbed it desperately. One leg slipped off the plank and swayed precariously over the edge. The railing shook with her unexpected weight but it held and she was able to haul herself to safety.

Behind her Jade had removed her boots and was stepping barefoot on to the wooden planks. She held out her arms for balance like a tightrope walker, then carefully raised one foot and swung it forwards. Sam envied the ease with which she seemed to move, but her face was tense with concentration. She waited impatiently for Jade to reach her, aware that each minute might be putting Kate in more danger.

'Gym was the only thing I could do at school,' Jade sighed when she finally made it to the other side. She bent down to put her boots back on and asked Sam, 'Are you ready?'

Sam nodded. After what she'd just done edging their way along the railing seemed easy. Each step brought them nearer to shore and to Kate. She couldn't fail now. When they got to the security gate Jade told her, 'Here, lower your legs through here. I'll go first. Just copy me.' Sam watched her lower herself down to a metal support that ran diagonally from the walkway across to one of the pier legs. 'Hang on to the edge like this, then swing across to the other side. Are you ready? Go on. Now.'

Sam gulped as she lowered herself over the edge. Her legs seemed to sway through space for ages before she managed to find the metal support. It took all her courage to let go with one hand and reach out to the other side. Her body felt impossibly stretched and she feared she wouldn't make it. She could neither go forward nor back. She imagined herself suspended there until her grip weakened and she could hold on no longer. Then she thought of Kate. Kate needed her.

She brought her arm back and inched nearer to the gate before trying again. Somehow she found a new strength and managed to reach across to the rung at the other side. She clung to it desperately while her heart pounded and she struggled for air. The surface of the metal was corroded with rust. Her palms stung but she knew she wouldn't slip now.

'Here, take my hand,' Jade said as she helped her up on to the walkway.

Her legs were shaking when she finally got to her feet but she was filled with a sense of achievement that she'd never experienced before.

'Hurry,' Sam shouted, breaking into a run. 'I hope we're not too late.'

'So do I,' Jade agreed.

29

As Kate closed the street door behind her she could hear raised voices from the old lady's flat. She hurried up the first flight of stairs, anxious to avoid anyone who might question her. Water still squelched in her wet boots and she was dying to change into dry shoes. Someone must have been cleaning because there was a smell of flowers she hadn't noticed before. It seemed to get stronger the higher she went.

She didn't want to think about what she might find. She wanted to believe Sam, wanted to believe there was a ghost, but if she was honest with herself, she wasn't really convinced. She didn't know exactly what she was going to do. She hadn't a plan, but she was sure she'd think of something. Yet, when she reached Sam's door, her hand faltered. She couldn't get the key in the lock and when she did, it wouldn't turn easily. The party suddenly seemed a very long way away and she was aware how big and empty the house was. At least Sam was safe. She imagined her enjoying herself. She was sure she wouldn't have missed her yet.

She grasped the key and turned it determinedly in the lock. She heard the click as the mechanism gave and the door slowly opened. Was that someone crying? No, just her ears playing tricks on her. It was very cold in here. She'd have to find a sweater to put over her skimpy top. What was that? No, nothing, only the stair light switching itself off. She felt around for the light switch. Where was it? It was so dark she couldn't see a thing. Her own breathing sounded strange and eerie in the silence. It was her own breathing, wasn't it? Suddenly she didn't feel so sure. She was thankful when her fingers finally found the switch and the room was instantly flooded with light.

She decided to check the whole flat. If anyone was playing tricks on Sam she'd find the evidence. She wasn't afraid, she told herself, over and over, as she quickly pulled a sweater over her head. Her arms were covered with goose bumps and she couldn't stop shivering. The corridor seemed very, very dark. Even when she switched on the light it remained dismal. She hurried down it and looked into the kitchen. Everything was just as they'd left it. She put the dishes into the sink and switched on the kettle. Now she was here she felt strangely unwilling to go back out into the corridor. She knew that was ridiculous. It would take less than a minute to check every room, then she could relax.

She looked at the light bulb warily. It seemed so dark in the corridor she thought something was wrong. Now the bathroom. There was nothing suspicious there. Only the bedrooms to go. She could hear the kettle boiling and was tempted to turn back. A hot drink would soon stop her shivering. She hurried to the bedrooms, eager to get it over. Both doors were closed. She turned the handle on the door to the spare room but it seemed to be stuck. She imagined someone at the other side, holding it fast. But that was absurd. It was just that her fingers were too cold to function properly. And if someone was there, she was ready. She wasn't afraid. She'd think of something. There was that flowery smell again. Maybe it was Sam's perfume, but she hadn't noticed it earlier. It seemed to be getting stronger. Kate had never felt so cold. She must have caught something. She had to steady her hand to stop it shivering as she finally opened the door.

30

'Kate,' Sam shouted. 'Kate, where are you?' She was breathless from running up the stairs. There was no sign of her sister anywhere. Jade stood silently by her side, looking around the brightly lit room. 'She must be here,' Sam told her. 'The light's on. The door's open. It wasn't like that when we left. Kate, why did you do it?' She was sounding more and more desperate.

'We'll find her, don't worry,' Jade said grimly, leading the way into the corridor.

The whole flat was silent, waiting. The corridor had never seemed longer.

'Let me,' Sam whispered, her eyes glued to the door of the spare room. She felt an icy shiver run down her spine as she put her hand on the door knob. What was waiting on the other side? 'Kate?' she called.

She was answered by a faint moan from behind the door. She wrenched the door open and rushed into the room. Kate was lying on the floor. Her tights were torn and the skin on her knees was bruised and raw. Relief and horror flooded over her.

'Kate, thank God. Are you all right? What happened?'

They helped her sit up. She looked around her vaguely. 'I don't know. I'm not sure. I remember opening the door . . . then . . . I think someone pushed me, or something . . . '

'Don't worry about it now. You're safe. That's all that matters. Let's get out of here. This is Jade. Without her help I wouldn't be here.'

'Hi,' Kate said, taking her in for the first time. 'I feel so stupid. And cold. You're right, let's get out of this room.' She got to her feet easily and hugged her arms around herself. 'You can't stay here, Sam.'

'I have to. I can't just give up. What can we do? How can we help her?' she asked Jade, as they entered the kitchen.

'I'm not sure. We don't know what we're dealing with yet. Whatever it is, it seems to be getting stronger.'

'We have to try.'

'No, it's too dangerous,' Kate insisted. 'You have to find somewhere else to stay.'

'Mrs Armstrong swore she wasn't dangerous.' Sam was puzzled. Grace's was a sad, tragic story. She couldn't be evil, could she? 'Are you sure you can't remember anything else, Kate?'

'I came in . . . ' she started slowly.

'But why?' Sam interrupted her. 'You promised me you'd—'

'Don't nag, Sam. As I was telling you, I got here. It was dark and really quiet. I decided to search all the rooms, make sure no one was playing tricks on you. I went down the corridor. I remember feeling very cold. I was sure someone was there, hiding behind the door.'

'Then what happened?' Jade asked. 'Try and remember everything. It could be important.'

'The door was stuck. I had to force it open. I walked in,

switched on the light. I couldn't believe it. No one was there. Nothing. The room was totally empty. I checked the window, but no one could get in or out that way. Then the door slammed shut behind me. Next thing I knew something pushed me across the room. I remember falling and . . . I don't know. I must have been unconscious. I had this strange feeling of sinking. There was cold water closing over me. I felt so far away from everything. It was weird. Then, the next thing I remember, I heard your voices.' She looked from one to the other. 'I'm sorry. I can't remember anything else.'

'Don't worry about it now,' Sam told her, putting her arm around her shoulders. 'You're safe. That's all that matters.'

'Yes,' Jade agreed. 'If we hadn't arrived, who knows?' She shrugged and turned to Sam. 'Where's that crystal I gave you?'

'I think it's in my jacket. I'll go and get it.'

Jade waited until Sam was out of earshot then asked quietly, 'Are you sure that's everything? If you're holding anything back you must tell me. I need to know.'

Kate looked at her thoughtfully. There was a moment's hesitation before she said, 'Yes, there was something. Something really . . . well, crazy. I thought I saw photos on the wall. But there aren't . . . ' She stopped suddenly as Sam came back into the kitchen. She looked puzzled.

'I can't find it,' she said.

'I told you to keep it with you,' Jade said crossly. 'Where did you have it last?'

'It was in my pocket.'

'Don't fight,' Kate pleaded. 'We'll find it.'

'We'd better. I need it to seal the room.'

'Maybe it's too late for that,' Sam said sadly.

They finally found the amethyst crystal under one of the chairs in the living room.

'What are you going to do?' Kate asked Jade. Her eyes were bright and enthusiastic again.

Jade had taken a leather thong from her velvet bag and was knotting it round the crystal. 'I'm going to try and seal the door with this. That seems to be where the energies are strongest. We can't do anything else tonight.'

A few minutes later they closed the front door behind them. The sound seemed to echo through the empty flat for an impossibly long time. The three girls looked at each other and shuddered as another noise reached them. The sound of a door banging as if caught in a sudden draught.

'Did you . . . ?' Sam began to say.

Jade shook her head. 'Hurry. I'll tell you later.'

As they started down the stairs the lights suddenly went out. Sam felt for the switch but nothing happened. She grabbed Kate's arm and together they crept down the dark stairs and out into the night. Once in the street they looked up.

'Is that . . . ?' Kate whispered.

'Yes,' Sam replied. 'It's the room.'

'But we didn't . . . '

They all stared up at the window for a moment. It was long after midnight and the whole house was in darkness. Except for the flicker of candlelight on the top floor. Only something was blocking the light. Framed in the window like a great dark shadow, was a human silhouette.

31

Sam had never known such a long night. She felt she'd aged a year while she tossed and turned on the cold, hard floor of Jade's beach hut. The few times she'd managed to drift off to sleep her dreams had been even worse than reality. She couldn't remember much, except there was always water. Always cold, stagnant, threatening. The party on the pier went on all night and the music reminded her of what she was missing. She supposed Grace hadn't experienced many parties either in her short life.

It was after midday when Ben came running up to them as they tried to warm themselves by the newly laid fire. He was still filled with energy from the party, although his face looked tired and drawn. 'What happened to you?' he asked casually, while Hobo bounded over to greet them. 'Is something wrong?'

Sam looked up. She was white as a ghost herself.

'It was all my fault,' Kate admitted.

'What?'

'No, it wasn't. You didn't start anything,' Sam reassured her.

'Start what? What's happened?' Ben asked crossly.

'We found her unconscious on the floor,' Sam told him.

'I can't explain. I was trying to help. I went into that room and . . . ' She looked at Sam pleadingly.

'We think Grace attacked her.'

'Grace? You saw her?'

'No, not exactly. I didn't see anything but . . . '

'Then you can't be sure, can you?' Ben said very quietly.

'There is something wrong in that house,' Jade insisted.

'Yes, there is,' Ben agreed. 'Gran's really upset, Jonathon's on the warpath.'

'That's why we've got to do something. We've got to help her or she will end up in a home,' Sam said gently.

'Don't you think you've done enough already? The house was fine until you moved in.'

'That's not fair,' Sam protested.

'You're obsessed with Grace.'

'Stop it,' Kate shouted.

'Yes, fighting won't solve anything,' Jade told them.

Ben turned away and Sam feared he was about to storm off, but in the end he only put some more wood on the fire and started to encourage the flames. Smoke seeped from the surface of the wood before it finally burst into life. Sparks shot out with an unexpected ferocity, causing Hobo to withdraw to a safe distance.

'It's all ancient history,' Ben said at last.

'Not any more,' Sam told him sadly. 'We have to do something. It's already started. We have to finish it.'

'What can we do?'

'We have to find out what Grace wants. Why she can't or won't leave,' Jade answered.

'More than that, we have to help her. We have to set her free,' Sam insisted.

32

'Gran,' Ben said gently, 'are you sure you've told us everything?' It was late Sunday afternoon and they were sitting in Mrs Armstrong's living room. The bruises from her fall looked worse than ever, making her seem even more frail than usual.

'I have told you. Grace would never hurt anyone. You won't send her away will you? This is her home.' The old lady looked pleadingly at them all.

'What if she wants to leave?' Sam asked softly. 'If I were her, I'd want to get away from a place where I'd been so unhappy.'

Mrs Armstrong sighed. She fumbled in her bag and produced the photo of Grace and her fiancé. 'I did my best,' she said sadly. 'I tried, I really did.' Sam knew she wasn't talking to them any more. It was Grace she was trying to convince.

'Don't upset yourself, Gran,' Ben told her. He took her hand and stroked it gently.

The old lady shook her head and put the photo away. 'Leave the past be,' she said at last. 'What's done is done. It can't be changed now. Maybe Jonathon was right. I should never have rented out that flat.'

'Don't blame yourself. It's not your fault,' Sam assured her.

Mrs Armstrong just looked at her and shook her head. 'I only wanted her to be happy. I'd never do anything to hurt her.'

'Of course you wouldn't. Neither will I, I promise you that, but the past needs to be laid to rest. And so does Grace.'

They left a few minutes later and walked slowly up to the top floor.

'You'd better stay in Hope's flat tonight,' Ben said. 'I've got the key.'

'OK. Hopefully by tomorrow things will be settled one way or another. I'll just go and get a few things.'

'Not on your own, you won't,' Kate insisted. 'Come on, Ben, it's your family and your bloody ghost.'

'Kate!' Sam complained.

'No, she's right. I never liked going into that flat. There were always rumours about it. Hobo doesn't like it either. Let's get it over with.'

Sam held the key tightly in her hand, remembering how happy she'd been that day she'd arrived just two weeks ago. It felt much longer. She'd been through so much since then, and whatever happened, she knew she wasn't going back.

'Wait for me,' Kate ordered as Sam left the living room. 'You too, Ben. We're all staying together.'

'I won't miss this corridor,' Sam told them.

'Look, what's that?' Kate whispered, pointing to the floor.

'It's broken glass,' Ben said.

'No it isn't.' Sam picked up the leather thong that was hanging from the door knob of the boxroom. 'It's what's left of the crystal.'

They all shivered. The dull blue carpet was covered with tiny fragments of glittering amethyst as if something had tried to smash it into a thousand pieces.

'But what could do . . . ?' Ben whispered.

'Ssh, not now,' Sam ordered. It had suddenly gone very cold again and she didn't want to waste any time. She pushed open her bedroom door and stared at the scene before her. The window was wide open and the curtains billowed into furious shapes.

'At least that explains why it's so cold,' Kate said brightly.

'But it doesn't explain this.'

They looked at the chaos in the room. Someone, or something, had emptied all the drawers and thrown all the clothes from the wardrobe. The clock that had stood by her bedside had been smashed against a wall but, otherwise, nothing seemed to have been damaged.

'Get the bedding, will you,' Sam said as she started to shove clothes into a carrier bag.

'It must be Jonathon,' Ben said. 'I'm sure he's got a key.'

'I'd like to meet him. I've got a few things to say to him,' Kate told him, as she rolled up the duvet.

'You've always got something to say, haven't you?' Ben snapped.

'Stop it, you two. Let's get out of here as quickly as possible. Wait a minute, Kate, you've dropped something.'

'What is it?'

'Here, see for yourself.'

Kate stared at the piece of paper Sam gave her. It was a small, square photograph of two little girls playing on the sand, building a dam to hold back the tide. They were dressed in surprisingly formal clothes that looked far too uncomfortable for the beach.

'Is it her?' Kate whispered.

'It must be. I've never seen it before,' Sam told her.

In the background you could just see the pier, with a crowd of people leaning over the railings. But what really caught Sam's attention was the way the two girls were gazing at the camera. They looked so solemn and intense, as though they'd seen through the veils of time and were aware of everything that the fates had planned.

33

Back in Hope's flat, the minutes dragged by while they waited for Jade. Ben seemed increasingly ill at ease. He scowled whenever anyone spoke to him and his replies were monosyllabic grunts.

'I don't like this any more than you do,' Sam said, trying to draw him out, 'but I have to do something. It can't go on like this. We have to finish it.'

'Maybe you're playing straight into Jonathon's hands. He's set this up and you've fallen for it.'

Kate began to protest but Sam got in first. 'No, Grace was here. I saw her.'

'That's the problem. You talk about her as if she was real. And now Gran believes it too.'

'We're trying to help,' Kate said angrily.

'With a few crystals and a bit of mumbo-jumbo. Do you really think that's going to work?'

'I don't know,' Sam said simply.

'No, you don't. You're meddling in things you know nothing about.'

'So you've got a better idea?' Sam snapped. 'We all just sit here and do nothing? Is that it?' They glared at each other angrily. 'If you're not prepared to help, you'd better go.'

'OK, I have to feed Hobo. I'll be around, if you change your mind.' He got to his feet and walked slowly to the door. 'Take care,' he said.

'We'll talk more tomorrow. And don't worry about Jonathon. He doesn't know anything about this.'

Sam listened to the sound of his receding footsteps with a heavy heart. Why did everything have to be so difficult? Just for once, couldn't something go right? There'd be plenty of time to sort things out with Ben later. Now she needed to focus her mind for the evening ahead. Everything would be different tomorrow.

Jade returned to the house just before sunset. She was wearing a long scarf wound round her hair and an old Arran sweater over her thin cotton trousers. She began to empty the contents of her velvet bag on to a scarf she'd spread on the floor in Hope's flat. Among the assortment of crystals there were some bundles of dried herbs, candles, a few small mirrors, and a set of wind chimes.

'No crucifix and holy water?' Kate said, looking disappointed. 'They always have them in the movies.'

Sam gave her an exasperated look. 'Are you ready?' she asked Jade.

'If you are.' Jade was sprinkling coloured water from a small bottle over each crystal in turn. 'Are you sure you want to take the risk?'

'What risk? Sam . . . ' Kate began.

'No, let me speak,' Sam insisted. 'This is something I have to do. There's some link between me and her. I am involved. I can't run away from this.'

'But why you?' Kate asked unhappily.

'Because I know what it's like to be without hope. Don't

forget all those months I spent shut in my room. There were times when I was stuck in a black hole of despair. I thought things would never get any better.'

'Why didn't you say anything?' Kate said with tears in her eyes.

'Because no one could help. Because I wanted to spare you. If I'd had the strength I might have killed myself.' She stopped as the memories came flooding back.

'Don't,' Jade cautioned, taking her hand. 'Don't give in to the darkness. If we go up there, we all have to be strong. The sickness has been festering in this house for a long time. Don't show it any weakness. Can you do that?'

Sam looked at her solemnly. 'I don't know,' she said. 'I'm just not sure.'

'We don't have to do anything,' Kate said. 'We don't even have to stay here tonight. We can find a B&B. Don't take any risks, please, Sam.'

Sam smiled. 'I never thought I'd hear you say that. I have to see it through, but you don't. I'd never forgive myself if anything happened to you.'

'And you think I would? If you're going up there, so am I. I'm not scared.'

Sam gave a huge sigh. 'I am. We don't know what's waiting for us. Maybe I'm not strong enough, but I have to find out. If you're ready, Jade, let's go.'

'When we go in there, we have to trust each other totally,' said Jade. 'No one can leave until I say so, understood? Don't let anything distract you. There are powerful energies locked in that room. I don't know what's going to happen when we release them. No matter how scared you are, you have to stay put. Can you promise me that?'

Jade left them to their thoughts while she went ahead to prepare the room. They watched the clock anxiously as the seconds dragged by, listening intently for any sound from upstairs, but there was nothing. Their imaginations rushed in to fill the vacuum.

'What do you think she's doing?' Kate whispered.

'Ssh . . . ' Sam was still looking exhausted, but she seemed quite calm and in control. Maybe she was stronger than they'd all realized. Kate kept quiet obediently, although she was so wound up she could barely sit still.

At last, Jade returned and signalled them to follow. 'Remember, don't give in to the darkness. Just focus on the crystals, as long as you do that you should be safe.'

34

It seemed unnaturally dark as they walked up the final flight of stairs. Outside there were still the last remnants of daylight, but none of it had reached this far up the stairwell.

'Your eyes have to adjust,' Jade told them, refusing to switch on the electric light.

A strange smell met their nostrils as they pushed open the front door and they saw a bunch of herbs had been left smouldering on the coffee table, next to a group of night lights. Their flames seemed so small and insubstantial, barely able to hold back the shadows that crowded round the edge of the room.

As they approached the corridor a draught of cold air caused the curtains to billow and the candles to flicker as if they might go out. Sam and Kate looked at each other doubtfully, but the flames steadied and their eyes did adjust to the uncertain light. They gave each other a quick hug and crossed the threshold into the corridor. All the doors had been left open and they could see a night light burning in each room as they passed. Tonight the corridor didn't seem long enough. All too soon they arrived at the boxroom, feeling again that awful cold that always seemed to linger there. The door was closed and a bunch of dried herbs was pinned just above the handle.

Jade gestured to them to be silent. She handed each a crystal and showed them how to hold it. As she did so, she stared into their eyes as if trying to read their innermost thoughts. Sam fought off a moment's doubt. It was too late now to turn back. She took a deep breath and turned the handle of the door. Nothing happened. She tried again, becoming increasingly confused as the door still refused to open. She rubbed her hands as if it was the cold that was the problem, then tried again.

'It's locked,' she whispered. 'I don't have a key.'

As they stared at each other they heard a floorboard creak and a sudden smell of perfume filled the air. Sam felt as if an icy hand had just grabbed her spine and was twisting it into an impossible shape. She didn't even notice Jade bend down and stare into the keyhole.

'Don't worry,' she said grimly. 'This is one of the few skills I learned in the children's home.'

She took a long pin from her hair and fiddled at the lock for what seemed like minutes until it suddenly gave. Sam was surprised when a delicate tinkle of wind chimes drifted towards them as the door opened. The sound seemed to unlock her body too, so she was able to move easily. She felt a sudden surge of hope as she gazed around the small room. Jade had been busy here and everywhere she looked there were signs of her work. Three candles had been placed, unlit, at equal intervals on the floor, forming a triangle. The only light came from two tall candles which burned on the mantelpiece much as they had in Sam's vision. The spaces on the wall where photos had once hung had each been filled with small mirrors and thin strips of silver paper which reflected back the light in strange distorted forms.

Jade led each of them to one of the unlit candles on the

floor. She lit a taper and handed it to Sam. Sam held it for a moment, summoning all her strength and courage, then lit the candle in front of her. Jade passed the lighted taper to Kate who suppressed a nervous giggle and followed her sister's example. Everything seemed surreal to her now they were really here.

Jade had begun to chant. She reached into a pocket and brought out something which she pinned to the floor with a stone. Sam didn't need to look to realize what it was. It was the small, white glove which had heralded the first apparition of Grace. She tried not to look at it. Tried not to remember. Finally, Jade took her own position, lit her candle and completed the triangle. She sat cross-legged on the floor and held out the crystal on her palm, motioning to the others to copy her.

Now all the candles were lit, Sam could see there were small crystals all round the boundary of the room and along the window sill. They seemed to trap the candlelight and hold it in their centres. Despite herself, Sam felt her whole body relax. The glow of the crystals and the soft light of the candles transformed the space, filling the room with a sense of peace. Even the flowers that patterned the old wallpaper seemed to revive and become more real. Sam was aware of their colours gaining strength. She could even smell their delicious perfume. Jade's voice had become increasingly intrusive. She wished she would stop that infernal chanting. Why didn't she leave them in peace to listen to the sound of the waves? The sea was so calming, far more sympathetic than any human voice could be.

The crystal felt heavy in her hand. Looking down at it she was surprised by how fiercely it glowed. The room around her grew dim. Her eyes began to feel heavy and a soothing tiredness descended over her. The crystal was calling her, beckoning her to enter its own universe where she'd be as free as the wind and the waves. It was so cold in the room. Why hadn't she noticed before? Holding the crystal was like having a block of freezing ice in her palm. She had to put it down. She let her hand drop and the crystal rolled slowly over her fingers and dropped to the floor. A blast of wind rushed round the room causing the chimes to clatter wildly and the candles to flicker.

'Grace,' Sam whispered. 'I can see you now.'

35

'Stop it,' Kate shouted. 'Look at her. She's in some sort of trance.' She had jumped to her feet and had rushed over to Sam.

'Leave her,' Jade ordered. 'Don't you understand? If you wake her now you'll kill her.'

'I'll kill her! You're the one that got her into this. I knew we should leave this damned house. All this mumbo jumbo, she's not strong enough for all this.'

'You'd better pray she is,' Jade said quietly, 'because it's too late to stop now. Grace has her. We have to get her back.'

'Grace! Are you crazy? There's no Grace here. Well, let's see. Come on, Grace, show yourself. Come and join us if you dare. What's the matter? Scared?' Kate was shouting wildly. She held Sam by the shoulders, shaking her as she spoke.

'Stop it,' Jade hissed. She started to shiver uncontrollably. 'Don't you see it's the darkness? I warned you.'

'The darkness,' Kate repeated, less certain now. 'We'll see about that.'

She rushed over to the door and pressed the light switch. Light flooded into the room filling her with horror as she saw how pale and strange Sam looked. Then, unexpectedly, the bulb blew. The filaments gave a final splutter of light then darkness descended. The candles flickered wildly and went out. Even the streetlights outside grew dim as though some dark shadow was cutting them off from the rest of the world. The darkness was absolute. Suddenly they heard the door behind them open, then slam shut. Kate rushed over to her sister and held her protectively.

'Do something,' Kate whispered. She could barely see Jade.

'The crystal. We have to find it.'

An awful silence descended over the room as they searched. The chimes were still. Kate hardly dared breathe. At last, her hand touched something.

'I've got it.'

Reluctantly, she picked up the crystal and put it back in Sam's hand. She realized Jade was moving round the room, replacing the candles in their positions before lighting them again.

'What's that?' she whispered when her eyes had readjusted to the flickering light. Something glimmered faintly on the floor, just outside the boundary of their triangle. Kate put her finger down gingerly and touched it, feeling an icy cold shock go through her system. She squinted trying to see more clearly. It looked like a row of wet footprints, as though someone had circled round them seeking a way through.

Sam looked even paler than before. If anything happened to her she'd never forgive herself.

'Concentrate,' Jade hissed. 'It's the only way to call her back.'

Kate could hardly bear to sit still. It was taking ages. The air seemed tainted with the smoke from the candles. It was hard to see the edges of the room. Kate suddenly realized she could hear the sea. She imagined the tide coming in, churning up the sand and shifting great banks of pebbles as it refashioned the shore. Her lips tasted salty and her hair felt damp and limp. Where was she? She was no longer sure. The waves were so close, getting closer all the time. She felt so alone, so totally abandoned. A sob broke from her lips, in a voice that didn't sound like her own. Then a hand touched her cheek. She started, and looked up to see Sam staring at her.

'What happened?' Sam asked, stretching her stiff legs. 'Have I been asleep?'

'Yes,' Kate answered, 'but you're safe now.'

'Ssh . . . ' Jade ordered. 'Listen. She's coming.'

There was the unmistakable sound of slow, shuffling footsteps coming down the corridor. Kate grabbed Sam's hand. It was still as cold as ice. Oh no, not again, Sam thought as the chimes began to sound and the door handle slowly turned.

36

They stared, fascinated, as the door slowly swung open, exposing the figure that waited in the shadows. She could hear its laboured breathing, a harsh rasping sound that assaulted their ears. Why had she involved Kate in this? Sam couldn't bear to wait any longer. Instinctively she picked up the candle and rushed over to the doorway as the figure seemed to collapse over the threshold.

'Get out!' it croaked. 'Get out! What have you done?'

'Mrs Armstrong,' they cried in unison as the old lady righted herself on her walking frame. Her face was flushed and her breathing was still erratic. She shuffled further into the room, refusing all offers of help. She peered into the shadows, stopping in front of one of the small mirrors suspended from the wall.

'Grace?' she called.

'She's not here,' Sam said gently. 'Not now.'

Mrs Armstrong ignored her. She continued to go round the room. Her progress was painfully slow. The frame scraped over the floor inch by inch while her feet dragged after it. 'This is your room. It'll always be yours, as long as I live.'

'We're trying to help her,' Sam said. 'She wants to be free.'

Mrs Armstrong turned to Sam and gazed at her as if she didn't know who she was. 'You think I didn't try to help her? You don't understand. No one understands.' She was moving forward again. Her whole body shook with each frail step. 'All these years, I kept it for her. I kept my promise. I did everything I could. Do you hear me, Grace? I know you come back. Why don't you show yourself to me? I'm your sister, not her.'

'Take her out,' Jade said. 'There's nothing more we can do tonight.'

'Let's all get out,' Kate agreed. 'It's all over, isn't it?'

'No, I won't leave. You can't make me. I'm staying right here,' Mrs Armstrong insisted. 'Jonathon was right. I should never have rented this flat.'

'Why did you?' Sam asked.

'I thought you'd be company. I thought she'd like you. Now you've driven her away.' She slumped against the wall in despair.

'I'll get you a chair,' Sam told her.

'We can't just leave her here,' Kate protested.

'We can't force her to go. It is her house,' Sam said gently. 'It's what she wants. You can't always protect people, you know.'

37

Kate was unwilling to leave Sam, but eventually she was persuaded to go downstairs with Jade.

'I'll be down in five minutes,' Sam told her. Without bothering to close the front door, she walked back through the flat, blowing out the night lights as she went. The bunches of dried herbs were still smoking, filling the air with a pungent aroma of sage and lavender. She'd switched all the lights on and suddenly the flat looked empty and unlived in. She wouldn't be sorry to leave. She could hear Mrs Armstrong talking to herself as she went into her bedroom to get the armchair and a blanket. Would one blanket be enough, she wondered? It was still incredibly cold. She hoped she was doing the right thing. Perhaps she could persuade Mrs Armstrong to go home after all.

She dragged the chair across the corridor and had started to manoeuvre it through the boxroom door when Mrs Armstrong said, 'Come in, dear.' Sam was reassured. She sounded so much stronger. She gave the chair a final push and stepped into the room. 'There you are. Come in. Let me introduce you. This is my sister, Grace.'

Sam looked up in surprise. The candles had burned low and were smoking wildly. It seemed much warmer than before. The old lady must be wearing perfume because there was a sweet, heady scent in the air. But there was no one there.

She went over to Mrs Armstrong and tried to guide her to the chair.

'She wants me here, you know,' the old lady said happily. 'She needs me.'

'Of course she does,' Sam said gently. 'You are her sister.'

'I didn't know, you do believe me, don't you? I had no idea.' Mrs Armstrong gripped her arm with a surprising force. 'It wasn't my fault.'

'No, it wasn't anyone's fault,' Sam tried to reassure her as she draped the blanket round her shoulders.

'I think she believes you. Look, she's smiling. Look at her pretty hair.'

Sam couldn't stop herself from following Mrs Armstrong's gaze. There was a pool of water on the floor exactly where the small, white glove had been. The surface quivered as though touched by a sudden breeze and the reflected candlelight fractured into a myriad ripples. As the surface steadied a face began to form. She saw the golden hair, the fragile smile. No, she was mistaken. It was only her own face, her own dark hair reflected there. Grace wouldn't come back. The whole room was different, the atmosphere had changed. Jade had done it. The past was healed.

'I tried to stop mother,' Mrs Armstrong was saying. 'She burned everything. I saved what I could. Hid the dresses.' She began to giggle.

Sam left her while she went to get a spare bulb. The candles wouldn't last much longer. Even in the kitchen, she could still hear her laughing. The noise seemed to get louder and louder. Was that really the old lady? It sounded more like two children. Sam felt her feet faltering. She forced herself to go on. There was a glow of light coming from the boxroom, spilling out into the corridor and sweeping over her in a great golden wave. She had to shade her eyes from the light, yet even so, she couldn't focus properly. Everything seemed to be dissolving, the walls, the floor, the door and its frame. Her feet sank into the ground wherever they touched. It was a struggle to keep moving. Reality was constantly shifting around her like a field of long grass blowing in the wind.

She could just make out two silhouettes at the heart of the

disturbance. Were there two? It was hard to tell. They seemed to merge, separate, then merge again. There was a noise that could be wind, or sea, or simply the sound of the process of everything. Because Sam realized everything was in process; forming, disintegrating, reforming, in a permanent state of transition. Nothing was solid. Nothing lasted. But everything came round again. Like the two children, playing in the sand. It was no longer strange to see them. It seemed quite natural to watch them working together, building a dam to hold back the tide. Waves lapped gently at the heaped sand, finding a channel through, while their hands worked frantically to stem the flow. They looked up at Sam with solemn, wistful eyes. Water swirled round their ankles and splashed their skirts. They laughed gaily, then the taller one took the hand of the smaller and they began to fade away.

38

Sam was awake by dawn. She lay in Hope's bed listening to the first birds begin to usher in the new day. She dressed as silently as she could and crept past Kate who was still sound asleep on the living room sofa. She knew what she had to do, knew what she'd find when she went upstairs. She felt strangely peaceful. The whole house was peaceful now. It had changed. They'd done it.

She felt different too. She climbed the stairs easily as though her legs had gained a new strength. The early morning light flooded into the living room. It was a beautiful room. She'd paint it a nice colour, put up some pictures, make it her own. The sunlight spilled into the corridor filling it with an unexpected warmth, but it wasn't like her vision of the night before. Everything had returned to normal; the floor was solid beneath her feet. The walls were exactly where you expected them to be. The past was back where it belonged. The house was healed.

Mrs Armstrong was still sitting where she'd left her. There was a peaceful smile on her face. She'd slumped slightly to one side so one arm hung down towards the floor. Sam rearranged the blanket, tucking it gently round her knees. Not that it mattered. She wouldn't feel the cold now.

She went into her bedroom and took the photograph of the two girls from the chest of drawers. 'You're together now,' she told them, 'you don't need me any more.' She walked into the kitchen and lit one of the rings on the gas cooker. She took a last look at the two sisters. They were smiling now. They'd be smiling for eternity. Then she held the photo out and watched as the fire spread across its surface. The faces seemed to live on in the flames for a moment, then they too blackened and turned to ashes. Sam made herself a cup of coffee and sat and waited patiently for 8 o'clock. Then she dialled Jonathon's number and told him calmly, 'Mrs Armstrong's dead. You'd better come over.'

39

As Sam walked to the crematorium the following week she noticed how tired the trees were looking. The leaves seemed ready to drop at any moment. She stood outside the building and watched as the hearse arrived with the coffin. A large wreath of white roses was its sole ornament. In procession behind it, the sleek black cars that conveyed the family; Jonathon, Ben and his mother Hope, plus a few other relations she'd never met. Hope had arrived a few days ago. She was a tall, thin woman who wore turquoise and silver rings on every finger. Sam had noticed how she twisted one of them nervously round her finger as she talked, but it was Hope who'd invited her there, insisted that she come. She'd barely seen Ben since his grandmother's death. He'd avoided the house, or avoided her.

Today no one looked quite like themselves. Hope, dressed in a black suit, her hair pinned up tidily, seemed to have aged twenty years. She didn't look out of place next to Jonathon, conservative as ever in his dark suit and tie. Even Ben had been washed and groomed to a pale resemblance of his usual self. He looked uncomfortable in a new pair of jeans and a dark shirt. His sun-bleached hair was combed and tied back into a ponytail. They all stood and watched as the coffin was carried into the building, then turned stiffly and followed it. Sam noticed the wreath of white roses slip towards the edge but one of the bearers caught it before it fell. A lone petal fluttered to the ground and was carried away by the October breeze.

There were more people inside than she'd expected, many of them elderly. Sam took a seat near the back of the crematorium and listened as the vicar spoke of a long and happy life. She felt angry that he didn't mention Grace. It wasn't fair that her tragedy should be forgotten. As she looked around the room she realized there must be many forgotten stories here; stories that would simply pass away and die with their owners. Why did families do that? Why didn't they want to remember? Shutting things off, denying them, that was what caused all the trouble. No wonder Grace hadn't been able to rest in peace.

Suddenly she became aware of movement around her. The service was over already. People were getting to their feet, standing as the coffin slowly disappeared from view and curtains closed behind it. She noticed that the woman next to her was crying, but it was a gentle, human sound totally unlike the sobbing that had kept her awake so many nights. She watched the family walk slowly back up the aisle. Hope, supported by Ben, led the way, followed by Jonathon and a woman Sam took to be his estranged wife.

Back outside, people were milling around, shaking hands, offering condolences. Sam hoped to slip away unnoticed. She'd started to make her way through the cemetery when she heard footsteps on the gravel behind her. It was Hope.

'I'll walk with you,' she said, unpinning her hair. 'The family won't miss me for half an hour.'

Sam wondered if she should say something polite about the service but decided not to.

'Are you going back to Greece?' she asked instead.

'Next week, if I can. There's a lot of things to sort out. I can't leave it all to Jonathon.'

'What will happen to the house? Will you sell it?'

'Maybe. We haven't decided yet. We might just sell off the ground floor flat. Don't worry, we won't be making you homeless. We'll give you plenty of notice if we do decide to sell.'

They walked on in silence for a few minutes then Hope continued, 'There's something I want to show you. It's just over here.'

Just before they reached the main gate Hope stopped in front of a large war memorial which was still decorated with the faded poppy wreaths from the year before.

'He's listed in that middle section. Can you see?'

Sam knew immediately who she was talking about. She looked down the long list of inscribed names until she found it. Robert Oliver 1922–1942.

'They never recovered his body. That's all that remains of him.'

Sam shivered, thinking of the happy young man she'd seen in the photo.

'What about Grace?' she asked. 'Is she buried here too?'

Hope shook her head. 'No, she was cremated. Unusual in those days. I've no idea what happened to her ashes. My grandmother never talked about it. She never spoke her name.'

No, Sam thought. Of course she didn't. She didn't want to remember.

They stood in respectful silence for a few moments. Sam realized she might never have this chance to be alone with Hope again. 'I'm sorry,' she said quietly. 'About your mother. About everything.'

'At least she's not in a home. She would have hated that.'

Sam took a deep breath. She wasn't finished yet. There was one more question she had to ask. The hardest question of all. 'Do you believe I saw Grace?'

'Do I believe in ghosts? I don't know. I believe in misery and human cruelty. There's been plenty of that in that house. But it's all over now. I have you to thank for that.'

'You don't blame me?' Sam said quickly. 'If I hadn't moved in . . . '

'I think my mother needed to make her peace with Grace. You were just the catalyst. I think she'd made up her mind when she decided to rent the flat. Before she even met you.'

Hope glanced at her watch. Everyone would be back at the house now, wondering where she was. Someone would be handing round the sandwiches while Jonathon poured out sherry into the glasses the caterer had supplied. 'Let's sit over there for a few minutes, shall we?' She led Sam to a wooden bench that was sheltered by the boundary wall. A thick curtain of ivy covered the bricks, a few long tendrils spreading out to disturb the paving stones beneath their seat. There was one last secret she needed to share.

'My mother always blamed herself for Grace's death.'

'But it wasn't her fault.'

'No, of course not. If she'd been able to talk about it . . . If she'd had help . . . '

'There was no counselling then. It doesn't always help though,' Sam said, thinking of her own mixed experiences with mental health professionals.

'Don't forget my mother was only nineteen at the time. You can imagine what it was like for her when Grace's body was washed up. It had only been in the water for two days, but it was horribly disfigured. The pier was covered in barbed wire, in case the Germans invaded.'

'Her eyes,' Sam said softly.

'How do you know that?' Hope asked in surprise.

'I saw her, remember.'

They were both silent for a few minutes, each dwelling on an image they'd rather forget.

'My grandmother was a practical woman,' Hope continued at last. 'Believed there was no point dwelling on the past. Least said soonest mended, she used to say. She had Grace's room cleared out. Everything went. All the furniture, even the carpet. She forced my mother to help her. The day after the funeral they went through all her things. All the letters, old family photos, her diaries and old schoolbooks . . . they all went on the fire. Anything that could be burnt was. My mother managed to hide a few photos, determined to keep Grace's memory alive somehow.'

'And the dresses,' Sam added.

'Yes. She was lucky there. My grandmother had a bad headache that day. Left my mother to take all the clothes to the Salvation Army. She sorted out the dresses Grace had made herself and hid them at a friend's. Kept them there until her mother's death, twenty-five years later.'

'Why didn't she talk about Grace then?' Sam asked.

'I don't think she could. It'd been so long since anyone had even spoken her name. And she still felt guilty.'

'But why? It wasn't her fault.'

'No, of course it wasn't. She wasn't to know what Grace would do if she unlocked the room.'

Sam froze. 'You mean it was her? She was the one that opened the door?' Her eyes had suddenly filled with tears.

'Yes. She couldn't stand to see Grace suffer. She'd been locked in that room for weeks, refusing to eat. My mother said the crying was awful. She couldn't stand it any more. One night she managed to steal the key . . . '

'And Grace went straight to the West Pier and killed herself,' Sam finished the story for her.

'No one knew how she even got up there,' Hope said after a pause. 'She must have been desperate.'

'Yes,' Sam agreed. 'She was. But I think she's OK now.'

40

Two weeks later Sam sat in her living room looking at the cans of paint lined up on the floor. Kate was arriving with her parents the next morning to help her decorate. There was a pale shade of lilac for the living room, a rich pink for Grace's room. Somehow, it seemed fitting to choose a colour she knew she'd liked. She'd found a poster of roses too. Her father would take down the old shutters and fix up a new window blind. The room would be bright and cheerful, perfect for Kate. It was different already. That damp musty smell had gone. There was no more water appearing mysteriously on the floor. And the door behaved just like any old door. Sometimes it creaked a bit, but nothing that a few drops of oil on the hinges couldn't fix.

Hobo had fallen asleep on the couch. His long legs

stretched its entire length. As Sam watched they began to twitch, gently at first then more frantically as if running some dream race. He was much cleaner now. Hope had helped her get him into the bath a few days ago. They'd washed off years of grime, groomed out some of the tangles. It would be much harder to train him. He'd never been on a lead or had any kind of regular routine. Sam had never had a dog before, but she'd promised to look after him until Ben came back.

She looked at her watch. They'd probably be in the air now, Ben and Hope. Hope was taking him back to Greece for the winter, though Sam wasn't convinced he'd stay that long. She suspected that as soon as he began to feel stronger he'd be off, travelling again. He'd been more upset than anybody by his grandmother's death. At first he'd avoided Sam, then shouted at her, blaming her for everything. She hadn't been able to explain what had happened, to tell him what she'd seen. Then he'd been arrested when the police raided the squats. Found in possession of ecstasy. That was when Hope had stepped in.

The beach huts were all boarded up now, the area swept clean of debris and the remains of their campfires. Maxine, she knew, was spending the winter in a squat in East London; the others had dispersed all over the country. Even Jade would go soon. She couldn't just hang around the seafront all winter. Sam had offered to let her stay for a few weeks until she found somewhere else but Jade had refused. Brought up in institutions, she'd never had a proper home. She preferred the open air.

Hobo opened an eye and wagged his tail lazily. Four o'clock. Time for his walk, then supper. He got down from the couch clumsily, stretched and shook himself, then looked at her expectantly. He seemed completely at home. We're both at home, she thought happily as she went to fetch his lead.

41

A cold wind blew up from the sea reaching even into the doorway where Jade sheltered. It was long after midnight and the temperature had dropped to its lowest point. Jade eased her numb limbs. It was best to keep moving, she'd learned that from long experience. She'd made a bed as best she could from cardboard boxes, newspaper, and an old blanket. It wasn't too bad. She managed to drift off to sleep some of the time, even to dream. It was peaceful too. The streets deserted and free from traffic.

She curled up in a tight ball and pulled the blanket over her head. Soon she was far away. It was summer and the air was filled with the buzz of voices, happy, excited voices. A band began to play and she noticed people were dancing. It was like a scene from an old movie as the couples whirled around the dance floor. Above her head small flags were strung all round the room fluttering gaily in the warm sea breeze. Long trestle tables were laden with food and crockery. She knew she was in the concert hall, seeing it as it had been in happier times. She'd been here before. She'd had this dream almost every night recently. And she knew she wasn't alone. There was always someone else watching as if sharing the same dream. Someone else who would never dance in the sunshine, never taste the food, never tap her feet to the music.

As soon as it was dawn she got up and made her way to the seafront. It seemed as if she had the whole world to herself. She'd miss the sea, but she knew it was time to move on. There was one thing she had to do before she left. She walked barefoot to the water's edge and let the waves break round her feet. To her right the old pier seemed less decrepit in the gentle light of dawn. It looked deserted, but she knew if she waited long enough the other would come. Yes, there she was, just emerging from the old concert hall.

Jade opened the velvet bag where she kept her crystals and emptied them on to her palm. She watched them glitter, seeing in their rich colours some older, fiercer light. Her fingers closed over them. She loved the feel of their rough surfaces against her skin. As she stood there the sky slowly lightened and the sea filled with colour. It was time. Jade raised her arm and flung the crystals into the water. She saw them fall to the sea bed, imagined she could see them lying on the sand still alive with light and colour. In her mind's eye she followed them out to sea. The other had seen them too. She was leaning over the railing, watching, her summer dress billowing around her. As she turned away Jade thought she heard music coming from somewhere a long way away. 'Goodbye,' she whispered. Then she climbed the stairs to the main road, without ever looking back.

Other books by Hazel Riley

Thanis
ISBN 0 19 275127 1

Thanis smiled. 'I knew you were the one. I knew it from the beginning, but I had to make sure. Jessica, I have a commission for you.'

It is the chance of a lifetime, the lucky break that Jessica has always dreamed of, an opportunity to really make her name as an artist. It is only when Jessica arrives at the isolated house in Cornwall with the mysterious and enigmatic Thanis that she begins to have doubts. Why is the silver spiral that Jessica is to make so vital to Thanis? And will Jessica have to pay too high a price for her success?

'*Thanis* is gripping, mysterious and imaginative, and I couldn't put it down.'
> *The Bookseller*

'This seriously sinister novel is one of the most original and disturbing works of fiction I've read for some time. Highly recommended.'
> *School Librarian Journal*

'Imaginative and well written'
> *Junior Times*

'I thought this book was absolutely brilliant. I have read several best-sellers this year but this beats them hands down.'
> *Judge, Lancashire County Library, Children's Book of the Year 2001*